"You're the boss— what you say goes."

Gillian's words were taunting; she seemed unable to help herself.

Randall closed the gap, reaching for her wrist. "Does it? Suppose I said I intend to become your lover again?"

She shook her hand free, color swamping her cheeks, excitement increasing her heartbeats. "Don't be stupid! I happen to be engaged—to another man."

His arms linked around her, his lips touching hers. "We're so nearly lovers, my sweet one. Twice we've slept together...."

Twisting away, she answered, "'Nearly' is the important word. We aren't and we haven't."

She was pulled roughly against him, his mouth hard on hers, and unconsciously she was clinging as she used to do....

It ended differently now. He prized her hands from his shoulders and abruptly pushed her from him. "You're right—we're four years too late."

LILIAN PEAKE
is also the author of these

Harlequin Presents

157—THE DISTANT DREAM
166—FAMILIAR STRANGER
186—A BITTER LOVING
190—THIS MAN HER ENEMY
198—NO FRIEND OF MINE
206—THE LITTLE IMPOSTOR
213—SOMEWHERE TO LAY MY HEAD
225—A GIRL ALONE
229—PASSIONATE INVOLVEMENT
316—NO SECOND PARTING
330—ENEMY FROM THE PAST
341—RUN FOR YOUR LOVE
353—DANGEROUS DECEPTION
384—A RING FOR A FORTUNE
407—A SECRET AFFAIR
424—GREGG BARRATT'S WOMAN

and these

Harlequin Romances

1778—A SENSE OF BELONGING
1831—MASTER OF THE HOUSE
1855—THE IMPOSSIBLE MARRIAGE
1868—THE DREAM ON THE HILL
1900—MOONRISE OVER THE MOUNTAINS
1944—HEART IN THE SUNLIGHT
2220—REBEL IN LOVE
2279—STRANGER ON THE BEACH
2404—PROMISE AT MIDNIGHT

LILIAN PEAKE

strangers into lovers

Harlequin Books

TORONTO • LONDON • LOS ANGELES • AMSTERDAM
SYDNEY • HAMBURG • PARIS • STOCKHOLM • ATHENS • TOKYO

Harlequin Presents edition published September 1981
ISBN 0-373-10454-5

Original hardcover edition published in 1981
by Mills & Boon Limited

Printed in U.S.A.

CHAPTER ONE

THE passers-by stopped, gazed admiringly through the shop window, then went on their way. From her flat over the shop, Gillian looked down into the narrow side street. It was early on Monday morning and the 'Closed' sign had not yet been turned to 'Open'. Even when it was, few customers came in.

Everett's stock was good. He had a name in the town for reliability and honesty in his dealings. Even so, antiques were not a necessity of everyday life. People bought such things when there was money to spare; when they wanted something reliable in which to invest, or when they sincerely loved the articles, to which time and fine workmanship had added a patina, an elusive beauty.

Sighing, Gillian went down the stairs leading to the street, securing her personal entrance door behind her. What a pity, she thought as she unlocked the shop door, that there were no eager would-be customers following her in.

Everett had told her he would be away for most of the day. He had gone to London overnight, seeking new stock; the capital city was too far away from the bustling Dorset country town to crowd such a journey into one day. Gillian looked forward with contented expectation to his return. Their friendship, and subsequently their engagement, was warm and affectionate.

This was the way she wanted it. All her passion, all her capacity for rapturous loving had flared, roared and burnt itself out four years ago when she had been nineteen. The man she had loved had been eight years her senior. Her memory of him was like a shadow, intangible, without substance, but which followed her doggedly, blackly, wherever she went.

Now there was Everett, undemanding yet affectionate, understanding her restrained responses to his kisses, knowing about the passionate affair and accepting uncomplainingly the mark it had left on the whole of her life. He had an unhappy marriage behind him, his wife having divorced him.

The morning passed, as did most Monday mornings, without a single customer. Gillian dusted and polished, rearranged the window display and checked over the list of items stored in a back room and which were waiting their turn to go on display in the shop itself.

Turning the notice to 'Closed', she locked the shop door and entered her flat, taking her usual hour's lunch break. During the afternoon, one or two customers drifted in. Both were women, and both told Gillian that they were 'just looking'.

It was towards the end of the working day that Gillian experienced a feeling of unease, a sense of foreboding which came out of nowhere. Nowhere but her imagination, she told herself firmly, and continued typing a letter in the slightly claustrophobic office at the rear of the shop.

The desk was placed so that the mirror which was positioned above and in front of her told her if anyone had come in, their arrival unheard over the clatter of the typewriter. The mirror showed her, also, her own reflection, full-lipped, long-lashed almond-shaped eyes complementing the young, firm sweep of jaw to a tilted, rounded chin.

Her long fair hair was caught back in a knot. Her mouth had a ready smile for patrons and strangers alike. What those customers did not see, as they thought how charming she seemed, was the sadness in the depths of her sea-blue eyes.

The clang of the door chimes had her swinging her

chair and making her way into the shop. This time, however, it was different. The welcoming smile was in place, the familiar 'Can I help you?' on her lips, but the words were never spoken.

It was Everett who had come in. There was nothing unusual in that; the man who accompanied him was the cause of her racing heartbeats. One look at the stranger had plunged her right back into the past. She was nineteen and passionately in love, a love that had grown out of a look across the room at a party. Each had known that neither had belonged there, that each wanted to be alone, and alone—together.

The love had passed from hand-holding to kissing, to ardent embraces. There had been promises never to part, to live together and love together until their dying day. Four years ago she had, as she had thought, said goodbye to him for the last time, never, ever, to see him again.

Everett broke into Gillian's reverie. 'Dearest,' he said—he never called her 'darling'—'I'd like you to meet Randall West. We met by arrangement in London. He'd like to have a look round.'

Gillian had heard only half Everett's words. *We met by arrangement*. . . . After the party, in an eight-word exchange. He'd said, 'Tomorrow, three o'clock, outside the park café?' She had answered, 'Okay.'

She had been whisked off by the group with whom she had come. She assumed he had walked home alone; he was that type. Yet, she had thought, squashed between her friends in somebody's car, unbelievably he's chosen me to share his loneliness. And I chose him out of all the boys at that party, although we didn't speak one word to each other the whole evening!

He had seemed different, more withdrawn, older somehow than the others, which, at twenty-seven, he was. Had it been this that had made him stand out from the crowd? Or had it been his height, his detachment which she had found so attractive?

Now he was in his early thirties. The passing years, she decided, had not robbed him of that attractiveness. They had, if anything, intensified it, hardening his eyes, deepening the grooves running from long, straight nose to the full-lipped mouth.

His chin had firmed, while his high cheekbones imparted a lean, angled look to his features which spoke of experience gained and a maturity achieved. Of a facing up to life—and death.

'Miss Taylor.' His hand was offered. In the few seconds which elapsed before her response, it had registered that his voice, too, had sharpened. All warmth, all laughing indulgence had been stripped from it like bark pared from a tree. Their hands met, and a strange ache weighed down her arm at their first touch for four years.

There was another change—his blue eyes had lost their uncertainty and their desperation. Now they were ice chips, and decisive, seeing into the future, the incredible, attainable future. They signalled a message: *I have not forgiven you.* With speed, he released her hand.

'It's good of you to patronise our shop, Mr West.' Her voice had found a higher pitch, betraying her tension.

Looks were exchanged between Everett Bushell and his visitor. Raised eyebrows had been the question, Everett's barely noticeable negative shake of his head the reply. Randall West turned back to Gillian.

'Isn't it, Miss Taylor?' was his ironic answer.

'I'll get the books,' said Everett, leaving the shop by the street door and making for his own house.

Books? Gillian frowned. What books? Was that what Randall was after? Everett had some valuable volumes tucked away in a bookcase and she guessed that they were the books to which he had referred.

Hesitant, uncomprehending, she watched him

wander from table to cabinet to high-backed wooden chair. His back was to her and she could think of nothing to say to establish a link ... A link with whom? This person was a stranger. The man she had known had been thin, gaunt of face, arms reaching out to her in silent anguish. So what if the name was the same? The personality within had altered beyond recognition. She had nothing to say to him.

If he noticed her retreat into the office, he made no sign. He did not know that she could watch him through the mirror above the desk. He wore a business suit, had an assured air about him which spoke of affluence and influence. *Was he married?* The idea came as such a shock, she covered her face, elbow on desk.

Her other hand reached out blindly, to fasten on the picture of a smiling boy. Swiftly she turned it face down and slid it into a drawer, pushing it to the back. That was something he must never discover. She loved the child more than life itself.

After she had typed a few words, her back felt cold, as if a draught had crept in to irritate. Everett must have returned and she had not heard the bell. The man in the mirror had the face of Randall West. He filled the doorway, hands in jacket pockets. He was using the mirror, too. Their reflected eyes clashed and there was a time span of four years to cover, a thousand questions to ask. Not a word came from her lips. Each one was snared like a frightened animal by the stiffness of her throat muscles, stilled to lifelessness by the snapping accusation in his gaze.

'Rand,' she whispered, surprising herself. Had he heard the veiled plea? But she had been the one to sever the invisible knot that had bound them.

His harsh, answering, 'Well?' told her that there was not an atom of forgiveness in him for what she had done. I only did it, she wanted to cry, for your sake. ... Had she? Wasn't it true that she hadn't, in the circumstances, been able to face the future without. . . .

The doorbell clanged and an involuntary sigh of relief escaped from her. Randall West's smile was taunting and brittle.

'We'll need your desk, Gillian,' Everett said. His smile was kindly, gentle, asking nothing in return. It went with his solidity of frame and with his sharing nature. He asked his fiancée not for love, but for affection, and it was affection he received.

Gillian rose at once, motioning to Everett to take her place. It was, however, Randall West who occupied the chair, at Everett's invitation. A quick smile from the visitor mocked her, bringing the colour of irritation to her face.

What was he doing there, anyway? Gillian paled when she saw the books to which Everett had referred. Those books had no antique value. How could they, when they were the company's books, relating to Everett James Bushell, antiques dealer?

'Everett,' Gillian asked, 'why are you—is he——?'

'Is it possible, Mr Bushell, for us to carry on our discussion in private?'

Colour tinted Gillian's white cheeks. 'I *am* Everett's fiancée, Mr West.'

'I'm aware of that, Miss Taylor.' Hard eyes found her left hand and dwelt momentarily on the turquoise and pearl ring she wore. 'You are not, however, part of the business.'

Everett looked uncomfortable, unwilling as he was to give pain to any fellow human being, even the pain of humiliation. Which personality asset, Gillian told herself acidly, his visitor most certainly did not possess.

'I'll go upstairs,' she announced with dignity. 'If a customer comes, Everett, call up to me, won't you?'

He smiled his gratitude at her discretion. Gillian wandered about her living-room, rearranging scatter cushions, twitching the curtains to a better hang. Her anxiety sought an outlet, her mind a way of grasping what had happened this afternoon—the reappearance in her life of the man to whom, four years before, she had, with total abandon, given her heart and soul.

Apprehension, also, followed her restless feet as they trod the patterned carpet. Was Everett making Randall a partner? Was he a new accountant brought by Everett from London? Or maybe some official sent by the tax authorities to inspect the books? Everett had told her recently that he had his worries about flagging sales. Had Randall come to investigate the reason for unpaid tax—except that she knew for certain that Everett was meticulous about such matters.

If Everett was offering Randall a partnership . . . Her hand went to her forehead. It would be an impossible situation. At the first opportunity she would have to tell Everett that this was the man out of her past. A shaking finger found the 'on' switch of her portable stereo cassette radio. The tape was playing her favourite songs. She sat at last, resting back against the couch, closing her eyes and seeking relaxation.

'Look around,' the singer was singing, 'and you'll find me there . . .' Her own love story had started and ended in her teens. It was history now, behind her, an episode which had enriched her life immeasurably and which could never be repeated. Tears trailed a glistening line to the corners of her mouth and she let them flow. She was alone, there was no one to see, to ask 'why?'

'Open your eyes, Gillian, and you'll find me there.'

She sat up, rubbing with the back of her hand at her cheeks. How long had he been watching her, treading with her the path of her thoughts? Once he had traversed that path beside her all the way. Since he remembered enough to continue to condemn her, he must remember everything else, too. Except for one thing he never knew.

Let me show you just how much I care. But it didn't last. She could tell that singer that it didn't last. If it did, why was this man looking at her now with such dislike? Her finger pressed the 'off' switch and the music stopped.

Finding her shoes with her feet, she stood unsteadily. Randall's hands were hooked by the thumbs to his trouser pockets. His head was slightly back, the angle narrowing his look as he inspected her, a faintly malicious lust in his eyes which must have been acquired in the intervening years.

He seemed to find the shape of her intriguing. He was unsparing of her feelings in his scrutiny, noting with an appreciative half-smile her swelling breasts beneath the neat working dress, the slender waist and hips.

'In three years plus, you've matured beyond my wildest imaginings. It couldn't have been my—activities alone which brought that about.' He paused and her stomach muscles tightened in terror. If he pursued the subject, discovered the cause . . . 'There must have been other men who brought about that change.'

The relief at his change of direction, which, had he pursued it, would have led him to the truth, was so great that she almost fainted. Far better, she told herself, to let him believe his own conjecture than to let him feel his way blindly to the events which had given rise to her maturity.

Inviting him to sit, she sank to the couch again. He joined her, lounging at the far end. There was a touch of familiarity in his smile for which she could not blame him. Once they had given their all to each other—more on her part than he would ever come to know.

'So after running from me, you became any man's woman.'

It was intended to provoke anger. Instead, the answer was a slow, sad shake of her head. She should have known, she told herself, that he would laugh at her denial. It was a harsh sound.

'Why aren't you honest?' he attacked. 'But it's not in you to be honest, is it?' His arms lifted, hands linking behind his fair hair—as fair as her own. 'You told me you loved me, and I believed you. We grabbed with both our hands at all life had to offer us. You gave me everything, telling me constantly that you loved me—then you ran away.'

If she told him why, her whole world would crumble.

He leaned forward, hands clasped loosely. 'In those first months, when I tried to find you, I went through hell. I wasn't allowed through the doorway of your parents' house. They even got your brother to push me away, although he did it reluctantly.'

Her hand covered her eyes as she murmured, 'Oh God, no!' Her younger brother, Martin, had been the only one she had told about her dates with Randall West. Her parents did not like her new friend, taking every opportunity to say so. This one is different, she wanted to tell them, but she knew they wouldn't listen.

He had bought her an ice cream from the café counter and they had wandered, hand in hand, round the small man-made boating lake. Once they stopped and gazed at their reflections. Even as she had stared, an oar from a rowing boat had smashed into Randall's floating shape. He had seemed to dissolve into a thousand ripples and—disappear. She had turned to him, hiding her face against his chest.

'You were dying, you told me,' she declared hoarsely, coming back from the past. 'You hadn't got much longer to live. That was why we—did what we did.'

'I was one of the lucky ones. Even at that time, I was having treatment with a new drug. I was beginning to hope.'

Her hands were shaking now as they rested against

her flushed cheeks. 'Why didn't you tell me?'

'I had to know for sure. It was one of those wonder drugs, but nobody knew much about it. I had this blood disorder which was killing me. I had nothing to lose and, as I thought at the time,' his glance sliced into her, 'everything to gain—including you. I was fortunate. On me, the drug worked. I was cured.'

'Oh, Randall, if I'd known——'

'I was cured,' he repeated, his mouth twisted, 'not only of the illness, but of you, too.' He leaned forward, anger in every strong line of him. 'You couldn't take it, could you, a relationship with a dying man. Why did you go? Afraid you might catch what I'd got, although I'd assured you it was neither infectious nor contagious? Or was it pity, not love as you said, that made you say "yes"? "Give him a taste of the joys of loving before he leaves this life." Was that what motivated you?'

'I could kill you for saying that!' she answered furiously.

'I died a death the day you went. For that I'll never forgive you.'

Gillian looked round desperately. 'Where's Everett?'

'Taken the books back to his house. He had a couple of phone calls to make.' There was a moment's silence. Gillian felt his eyes on her and she put up a hand to tidy stray lengths of hair that had escaped from the knot into which she had twisted the fine, fair strands.

Randall went on relentlessly. 'How long have you been engaged to Everett Bushell?'

'Nearly a year.'

'How does his lovemaking compare with mine? Do you respond the way you did to me? Do you tell him you love him, like you did me? That you couldn't live without him, that you'd give your own life if only it could save mine?'

Her hands over her ears did not shut out the implied accusations of treachery.

There were footsteps on the stairs and the door was opened. Everett hesitated, appearing to sense the tension, to feel the animosity which hung, like a low cloud, over the two of them. He frowned, looked from one to the other, then, in his mild way, asked, 'Have you made that tea yet, dearest?'

Gillian looked at him, surprised. 'I didn't know——'

'Sorry, Everett,' Randall apologised, equalling Everett's mildness. 'I forgot to pass on your message.'

Gillian was already in the adjoining kitchen, filling the kettle, switching it on. She was glad of something to do, working quickly, assembling crockery, taking milk from the fridge, anything to prevent her from thinking about Randall's biting indictment of her behaviour four years ago. Anything, too, to wipe away the enmity in his cold blue eyes.

As she made the tea she heard the words, 'the empty shop round the corner', 'solicitor', 'lease', 'immediate occupation'.

'It's larger,' Everett pointed out, 'which means the rent will be higher.'

'Naturally. That's to be expected.'

'So the shop's ours?' Everett queried. 'I mean—yours?'

Gillian appeared in the kitchen entrance, holding the tray. 'Will somebody tell me what's going on?'

There was a small silence. The men exchanged glances. Randall made as if to rise and take the tray from her. Everett, reminded of his position as host, jerked out of his chair and found a table on which to place the tray. Since his fiancée appeared fixed to the floor, he poured the tea. Gillian's heart thumped with an awful premonition. When she moved, it was like a robot acting out programmed messages.

Taking a cup from Everett, she sat in an armchair. Everett was now beside Randall on the couch. He looked at the visitor. 'I haven't wanted to worry her,' he explained.

Randall seemed to have no such scruples. He said to Gillian, his features and voice impersonal, 'Do you hold any financial stakes in Everett Bushell Antiques?'

'None at all. Why?'

Randall went on, 'So your sole interest is as the fiancée of the owner?'

'Yes. Plus my job. Why?' she asked again.

He enquired of Everett, 'Do I have your permission to tell her?' Everett nodded. 'The business, according to Everett's books, is not doing well. Outgoings are exceeding income and you must know what that means.'

Gillian turned agitatedly to her fiancé. 'That surely doesn't mean business won't pick up again. Most shopkeepers have their ups and downs. Things may be quiet at the moment——'

'They've been quiet for a long time, dearest. I'm certain you've noticed.'

'So where——' her heart was beating faster now, 'where does Randall—I mean, Mr West—come into it?' The familiar first name had slipped so easily from her tongue.

Randall, leaning back and watching her with hooded eyes, smiled at her attempts to minimise the seriousness of the situation, and thus eliminate him from the role he seemed about to play of rescuer from their financial difficulties.

'I'm offering your fiancé a deal, Miss Taylor, to help him out of his money troubles.'

Gillian's hand shook as she put down her half-empty cup. Everett sipped his tea, while Randall drained his and replaced the cup with a decisive clatter on the saucer.

'You mean,' she spoke to Everett again, 'he's going to be your partner?'

Everett replied, slightly on the defensive, 'He's

suggesting he buy me out.'

Gillian felt a surge of fear both for her fiancé's future and her own. If, as owner, Randall should decide that Everett's presence at the shop was, as former head of the business, inadvisable and asked him to leave, would Randall allow her to stay on? And if he did, would she be able to stand the strain of working for him? She sat back. Of course, the problem wouldn't even arise. If Everett left, she would leave, too.

'Something's troubling you, Miss Taylor. Maybe I could settle your doubts?'

Gillian found herself resenting his high-handed attitude. By the gleam in his eyes, she suspected it was deliberate. 'There's nothing in my thoughts, Mr West, nor my present, nor my future that you could help me with.'

The vehemence in her voice brought her fiancé's head round, and a humourless smile to the face of the man she had addressed.

'You can't escape me, Miss Taylor,' he declared, dangerously quietly. 'You see, Everett is staying on as the manager of the shop. If you go, he goes, too.'

Gillian did not accompany her fiancé and his visitor down the stairs. She waited at the window overlooking the street, watching as Randall talked at length to Everett.

Randall gestured towards the window, but she knew he could not see her through the patterned net curtains. Then he nodded in the direction of the main street which was round the corner from them. They were probably discussing the empty shop to which they had referred earlier. Her heart sank as she realised that, if the business was mooved into the High Street and the present shop sold, her own flat would go with it and she would be made homeless.

Her mind momentarily blanked out the possibility that she could suggest to Everett that, if they brought the date of their marriage forward, she would be able to move in with him as his wife. It did not, at that moment, seem strange to her that she had entirely forgotten her engagement and that she was thinking of herself as an unattached woman.

Pulling at the door, she raced down the stairs and came to a breathless stop beside them. 'You can't sell this shop,' she declared mutinously, addressing Randall West. 'It's my home. I'd have nowhere to go.'

Everett seemed too stunned by her outburst to find a ready reply. Randall glanced, frowning, from one to the other. He seemed to be wondering just what their relationship was if, as an engaged couple, the answer had not immediately occurred to them.

Everett offered eagerly, like someone having solved an almost insoluble problem, 'There's a flat over the other shop, too, isn't there, Mr West? Bigger than this one,' he addressed Gillian, 'so you would have more room. That is,' to Randall now, 'if Mr West is willing to allow you to rent it.'

Randall's eyes narrowed fractionally. 'At a higher rent, maybe I might. It depends.'

Memories of the past stirred and slithered, like a snake uncurling. He wouldn't—he couldn't mean. . . . 'On what?' She stared, daring him.

He smiled, as if guessing her thoughts. 'On whether I decided to continue to employ you.'

It had not occurred to her that he would seriously consider doing otherwise, and his vindictive attitude stunned her. 'But you said if I go, Everett goes. You couldn't——'

Everett placed a placating hand on her arm. 'Don't worry about such things yet. Where buying a business is concerned, events often move more slowly than you seem to imagine.'

'I think, Everett,' she said slowly, 'you might be underestimating Mr West's speed and ruthless efficiency where getting what he wants is concerned.'

Everett looked a little shocked. Randall smiled at Gillian faintly and humourlessly, as if daring her to confess her past to her fiancé. He already knows, she wanted to tell Randall; he knows, in fact, more than you do.

Slowly she returned to her apartment. There was one thing she had never told Everett—the name of the man from her past.

Their voices, drifting up, were clearly recognisable. Everett's was subdued, reasoning, holding a touch of deference. Randall's was authoritative, containing a hint of power, leashed but unmistakable. And from the way he was speaking it seemed to Gillian's over-sensitive ears that he was intent on taking over not only the business, but also their lives.

Once before she had put her life—and her future—into his hands. Was she prepared to allow that to happen again? She walked across to the large antique sideboard and picked up the photograph of her son. Then she replaced it.

The answer was obvious. She would tell Everett that Randall West was the father of her child. Once Everett knew, he would find another buyer for the business, and she would be left in peace again.

Even when Gillian told her fiancé about Randall West, it made no difference. In the past, he had been easy to manipulate and bring round to her way of thinking.

His past experience with a wife who, as he saw it, had let him down so badly by leaving him had put a shrug into his shoulders and a nodding acquiescence into his mind. Don't argue, his philosophy seemed to be. Agree to anything for the sake of peace and quiet.

On the matter of Randall West's takeover of the business, however, he was adamant. Gillian was both astonished and afraid. 'He's a forceful character,' she remonstrated. 'Already he has plans for making changes—fundamental ones, like finding a new shop——'

'It's something I've wanted for some time, dearest,' Everett told her gently, but with firmness. 'We simply haven't had the necessary cash.'

'But don't you see, he's changing more than that. He's even started to interfere with our lives. Mine, for instance. He's going to take away my home——'

'He'll give you another in exchange.'

Everett was being so reasonable about the whole thing she wanted to shake him! 'Not only that,' she persisted, seeking in her mind for persuasive reasons for eliminating Randall from their lives, 'he's not honest. He—he tells lies.'

Everett's puzzlement at her statement was genuine. 'When has he ever lied to you? In the past, I mean.'

Lied to me? Gillian thought, staring at the carpet. When, indeed, had he lied? About his illness? No, he had been so honest, so open about that, it hurt her even now to think about it. 'I can't recall the occasions exactly,' she answered evasively.

The reply had plainly not convinced Everett. 'I'm sorry, my dear, but there's no going back. The deal's on. Tomorrow we see a solicitor who will draw up the necessary papers. Even before signing them, Randall is handing over a large percentage of the price we've agreed on, and that, in my view, is extremely generous, not to say trusting.'

She reached out and put her hand over his. 'Anyone would trust you, Everett.' Affection, as well as gratitude at her belief in him, filled his answering smile. 'All this means, I suppose,' she persisted, 'that Everett Bushell Antiques becomes Randall West Antiques.' Everett nodded, and Gillian rested back against the armchair. Despite her seemingly relaxed position, the tension remained. 'Has he gone back to London?'

'He's staying in the town for a day or two. I offered him a room in my house, and he accepted.'

'You don't mean he's staying with you?'

He saw her dismay. 'You needn't see him if you don't want to. But,' he sat forward, saying hesitantly, 'if you could—well, see your way to forgetting the past—it's obvious he has—and offer him the hand of friendship——'

Gillian was shaking her head vigorously. 'I couldn't overcome in a few hours all the resentment I've felt against him these past four years. I'm sorry, but——' To her dismay, her voice wavered. It wasn't really resentment, she thought, it was love, but that was the one word she could not use.

'Gillian, my dearest!' Everett stood in front of her and pulled her up into his arms. They were comforting and undemanding and held her securely. He did not attempt to kiss her. Her head lay against his shoulder and the tears slowly dispersed, but the words lingered. 'Forget the past,' Everett had advised. 'It's obvious that he has. . . .'

Other words drifted in. *I was cured, not only of the illness, but of you.* Maybe his memory processes had blanked out their love. But the grudge he bore her for running out on him—would that ever go away?

CHAPTER TWO

It was Gillian's custom most evenings to go to Everett's place. They would watch television together, share a meal or simply read in companionable silence.

That evening, however, Everett had company—of a kind that would not welcome her appearance. And the man in question would no doubt take delight in telling her so. Deciding she would not give him the chance, she let herself out of her apartment and, instead of crossing the road to Everett's house, walked to the corner and into the main street.

As she climbed the hill, it occurred to her that she had not let Everett know she would not be coming, but she consoled herself with the thought that he was probably so deep in discussion with his visitor about the business deal, he would have forgotten her, anyway.

It was her favourite place she made for, through a short, narrow passage over which the walls of houses and cottages threw evening shadows. Opening out before her was a view she had grown to love. It stretched into the distance over Dorset and part of Wiltshire.

There were fields and hedgerows, trees coming into full leaf. Seating herself on a wooden bench, she let her gaze wander over the houses which climbed the hills and slopes. Some of them were cottages, while others were larger, varying in age and design.

As she gazed, she became conscious of being watched. Her head moved slowly to the right. Near the end of the walkway a man leant with his arms on the protective railings. He was not, like her, contemplating the view. His head was turned and his eyes stared fixedly, appraisingly, at her seated figure.

Even at that distance she recognised Randall. Her instinct was to rise and run, but her thoughts were diverted by the arrival of a family of four, two young children and their parents. One of them was a fair-haired boy, aged about three—Gary's age. His sister, probably three or four years his senior, chased him until the child made for the bench on which Gillian sat.

He clambered up and settled beside her. In a glance, the boy had summed up her smiling face. His sister started pulling at his arms, but he kept shouting, 'No, leave me, Lindy!' and shifted along the seat nearer to Gillian. With a shy look he silently implored sanctuary from his sister's pestering. The parents were gazing at the view, unconcerned about their children's squabbling.

The boy reminded Gillian so much of her own son, her arm automatically went round him. Thwarted, his sister lifted her shoulders and pulled them down, then gave up the chase, joining her mother and father.

The boy's eyes were staring and curious as, with complete trust, he studied Gillian's face. 'What's your name?' she asked.

'Duncan,' he informed her importantly. 'What's yours?' She told him. 'Are you a mummy?' he enquired, his perspicacity astonishing her. She nodded. 'Where is he?' He had, she noticed, assumed she had a son. To her relief, he did not wait for an answer. 'Where's his daddy?'

'He—he left us. He's—he's gone, gone for ever, I'm afraid.' If only she could have said, He's standing over there.

The child looked troubled. 'My daddy won't leave me. He won't go for ever!' The positive statement was also a plea. It was necessary to reassure him at once.

'Of course he won't. He loves you too much to do that.'

The boy smiled up at her as if in gratitude, wriggled off the seat and ran to join his family. Her one fear was that he would tell his parents in a loud voice that that lady sitting there was a mummy, too, but it was plain that by the time he reached them and his second quarrel with his sister was over, he had completely forgotten the incident.

A swift glance to her right told her that Randall had not moved from his indolent position against the railings. Nor had his eyes, which remained fixed on her. She was glad she had spoken quietly to the child and was certain, by Randall's cynical smile, that not one word of her secret had reached him.

Watching the family go—the boy ran ahead without a single look back—she did not notice that Randall had considerably narrowed the gap between them. He was standing beside her, hands in the pockets of his summerweight jacket. His eyes were on the view and, for a moment, she was able to study the profile which she knew so well—and would remember and love as long as there was breath inside her.

'Your fiancé was expecting you. He said you go across to him every evening.'

'Most evenings,' she answered, feeling his arm brush her shoulder and tensing at the contact.

He looked down at her, the fading light hiding his expression. 'What kept you away tonight? Me?' She did not answer, and he looked away. 'Never let it be said,' he drawled, 'that I would ever coonsciously be the cause of keeping lovers apart.'

'We're not lovers!' His eyes swung round to her again, and his look was frankly disbelieving. 'Everett isn't—like that.' She hated the amusement, which she guessed was at Everett's expense. 'He's been married and divorced. His wife left him, so now he's cautious about——'

'Where you're concerned, I don't blame him. It's no fun, believe me, taking an unstable, irresponsible woman into your life, and into your bed. The feeling when she walks out on you has to be experienced to be believed.'

It was almost impossible to swallow the lump in her throat. Unstable, irresponsible—when, by her action, she had proved herself to be the very opposite? But that was something he would never know. Abruptly she stood up and went to lean on the railings, hoping her sweeping gaze appeared absorbed enough to tell him she did not want his company.

When he joined her a few minutes later, her heart sank. She could not fence with him until sundown. Couldn't he see she wanted peace and quiet? For a long moment Randall, too, scanned the view. Then he said,

'I shall be coming to live in the town.'

Her head shot round. 'Why?'

Her question seemed to amuse him. 'Why not? I like the place, the whole area appeals. For a long time now, my fiancée has been urging me to look for a house in the country.'

Gillian caught her breath. Her hands grasped the rounded top of the railings, then she unclenched them so that he could not see her distress. She said, her voice high and falsely light, 'I'd have thought that by now you'd be married.' She turned, flicking back her head to flash him an artificial smile.

His narrowed eyes studied the long line from brow to chin, the wisps of hair which had escaped from the back fastening. 'Maybe, like Everett, I've grown cautious. Unlike him, I escaped the straitjacket of marriage, thank God,' he paused, seeming to enjoy watching her wince. 'But I got myself involved enough to live to regret it.'

Since he was now an engaged man, Gillian found his words puzzling. She turned back to the view but did not see it. For a moment the railings became her support, then her body, of its own volition, swung round and she found her feet retracing the path back to the narrow lane which led into the high street.

There were footsteps behind her, long, firm strides, then Randall was walking at her side. Keeping her face averted to gaze in the shop windows, she tried to ignore him, but their reflections threw the past back at her. All that was missing was his arm around her waist and her head on his shoulder. In those days, they had strolled, as if making the most of every second of their lives—their happiness, they'd thought, was agonisingly fleeting, the end a finality with which no human being could argue. Now they walked faster, and each step could only lead them to the inevitable, irrevocable parting of the ways.

Randall's hand fastening on her arm impelled her to a stop. He was pointing at vacant shop premises. 'This is ours now.' He was, she knew, being generous in using the word 'ours'. He really meant 'mine'.

Her eyes lifted. 'The flat above—is that the one I'm going to move into?'

They stood in front of the shop entrance. 'That depends,' he said as he had earlier, and Gillian looked at him sharply, prepared to be angry.

She saw his teasing glance and was swept back four years. The glimpse of the old Randall turned her heart over. 'No need to look for hidden meanings now, Gillian. There are two formidable obstacles between us that did not exist before—your engagement, and mine.'

She hoped he was too busy opening the shop door to see her swift embarrassment. The premises were so spacious they made even the thought of Everett's present shop seem claustrophobic. She nodded and said, as if speaking to herself, 'Much more display room, plenty of spaces in between for people to wander and browse. Is there good storage at the rear?'

'My word, we are well versed in retail display and management! You'll be making a bid for the top job

yourself soon, pushing your fiancé into second place.'
Gillian confronted him, face flushed, eyes flashing. 'Okay, so you haven't forgiven me, but you could at least treat me with respect and leave out the sarcasm.'
'Now that I can't guarantee. At least, not in private.'
She swung away from him. 'May I see the apartment upstairs?'
He led the way back through the shop's entrance and unlocked another door. There were stairs leading upwards and these he invited her to climb. 'Whether you approve or not,' Randall stated, following behind, 'you're moving in.'
They had reached the top where, lacking a light, it was dark. 'I thought "it depended".' She quoted his earlier statement.
He opened a door and the evening sun crept into the long, double-windowed living-room. Gillian reached automatically for a switch, but realised that the electricity must have been disconnected. She found it difficult to visualise the furniture in place; there would be so much space to fill.
'The condition is one which I don't think you'll object to.' Still he kept her in suspense, walking out of the room and opening another door. 'Bathroom, plus shower and so on.' The room was tiled in blue from floor to ceiling and her heart lifted.
The kitchen possessed everything a modern woman could wish for. The bedroom was large, too, and the decorations tasteful. Opening off this was a small shower room.
Gillian could not keep her delight from showing. 'I couldn't ask for more.'
'Except a man to share it with?'
The mockery was there again, but she would not let it needle her. 'Please tell me this condition,' she said evenly.

Randall led the way into a smaller room and stood at the door. As she passed in front of him, her shoulder brushed his chest and she tensed in self-defence as feelings which had been dormant for years threatened to swamp her.

Following her in, Randall stated, 'That this room should be my office. I'd have a desk, telephones, shelves fixed, filing cabinets installed.'

Her blue eyes met his calmly and she secretly wondered at her own control. Randall working here, coming and going as he wanted? The pleasure of his presence, the agony of having to keep her distance, the torment of knowing the barriers could never again come down between them?

Despite such doubts, she told him, her voice steady, 'I have no objections, none at all.'

'Good.' His intense gaze held hers and Gillian caught her breath as she heard, yet did not hear, a question which seemed to hover on the still air.

'That—that living-room,' she said, and time moved on again. Turning quickly, she made her way towards the room, her lungs working as though she had been running.

'What's wrong with it?'

'It—it's so big.' She looked at the bare floorboards. 'All that will need carpeting, and I refuse to ask Everett for money.' She forced a laugh. 'It'll have to be scatter-rugs or newspaper.' She smiled up at him. 'What a choice!'

He did not smile back. 'As landlord and owner, I shall furnish the place. I have the money, Gillian. I'm buying Everett Bushell's shop as an investment. My real work is leading a team researching into possible new sources of energy. I work for a multi-national company and travel abroad a great deal. I've recently returned from Canada.'

He walked to the window and gazed along the main street. The lamps threw their light across the road, casting a glow into the unlighted room. 'I'm glad you've done so well, Rand,' Gillian said softly. 'And—and thanks for all you've done to help—Everett and myself, I mean.'

He turned, putting his back to the windowsill, and against the yellow street lighting Gillian saw his shoulders lift and fall. 'I owe you a lot, anyway. I gave you nothing in the old days.'

'Don't say that!' It was a cry of anguish. 'I did—what I did for—for love, not money.'

'I didn't mean to insult you.' He approached her, his firm, strong body a black outline. With the outside light streaming on to her face, he must have seen her wide-eyed gaze, the parted lips, the short intakes of breath as she waited, wondered, her body tense with apprehension. If he touched her. . . .

A curled forefinger lifted her chin. Eyes hidden by shadow contemplated each illuminated feature of her face. His other hand held her shoulder. Her hair was stroked, a finger ran down her cheek. And I'm doing nothing, she thought, nothing to stop him.

The darkness was a veil misting reality, giving the present a nebulous, dream-like quality. When his hands moved from her throat to her armpits, then slipped down to outline her breasts, lingering as if to remind himself of their shape and young fullness, she stiffened. It's not the past, she argued with the dream, it's now, and I'm to marry another man. . . . Again his hands moved, outlining her narrow waist, broadening out to the greater maturity of her hips.

Again they lingered, and through the pressure of his palms she could feel the questioning of his probing mind. 'The same, but different,' she heard him murmur, 'different in an indefinable way.'

She compressed her lips to stop them from blurting out the truth. *I had your baby, that's what's different!* There was nothing she could do but stare up at him, willing him not to guess the truth.

'Different,' he muttered again. 'In this, too?'

His arms came round her with such gentleness she did not resist. His lips lowered and her head tipped back to receive them. The past was taking over again and it was as if they were still lovers. The kiss was an exploration, mouth upon mouth, touching, parting, only to touch again. Was it also a testing—of her reaction?

It must have been, since a moment later his embrace had hardened, his mouth had grown rough and insistent, all tenderness gone. The discovery of the maturing of her body into the fullness of womanhood seemed to have angered him. His kisses showed her that in her absence he had certainly not remained celibate but had gained experience of the kind which put fear in her heart as well as fuel to her simmering desires.

At the moment when, all reserve gone, she began returning his kisses, he pulled free of her clinging arms and thrust her from him. 'Rand?' she whispered, bewildered by his action, wrapped around as she still was by past dreams and fantasies. His words dragged her cruelly into the present.

'Is Everett keeping you so starved of physical love,' he snarled, 'you'd even come back to me as my lover for the satisfaction he deprives you of?'

In the semi-darkness she lifted her pain-glazed eyes to him. 'I could never love you now,' she returned, her voice intense and low. 'You've altered so much, you're more a stranger to me than a passer-by in the street.'

'So you were kissing me back out of pure reflex? Or were you imagining I was your fiancé?'

'Neither, Rand. I was kissing the shadow of a man, a loving and wonderful man I once knew. He'll never come back, I know that now. You see, Rand, not only were you cured of me; I was cured of you, too.'

The lie came from dry, stiffened lips—lips which still throbbed with his hard, meaningless kisses. She left him standing in the empty, unlighted room. Her footsteps echoed hollowly across the quiet street that led her back home.

Everett came into the shop next morning while Gillian typed a letter to a friend.

There was no other paperwork for her to attend to; the morning post had consisted solely of advertising material. Swinging round and anticipating a customer, Gillian saw Randall filling the shop doorway. Everett bent to give her a swift 'good morning' kiss, and as he straightened, Gillian saw Randall's fleeting, sardonic smile.

'We're off down the road to see the solicitor and finalise the deal,' Everett explained, his smile gentle.

'Everett,' Gillian felt she must make a last-minute appeal, 'are you sure we couldn't manage on our own, without outside help? When things are bad, they can only get better, surely? It may take time, but——'

Everett was already shaking his head. 'We've got two alternatives, dearest. Either we sell or we go bankrupt.'

'The business is as good as mine, Miss Taylor,' Randall informed her from the door. 'In about half an hour's time, both Everett and you will be employed by me. He has no objections. Have you?' She could only stare expressionlessly at him. 'Because if you have, you know what to do—leave.' His glance was cold as it skimmed her neat figure. He turned to go. 'Coming, Everett?' Everett followed.

Leaning forward among the antiques displayed in the window, Gillian watched the men disappear round the corner into the high street. A customer hovered, studying the articles on show. The woman's eyes came to rest on the display stand of jewellery. Anxious not to seem over-eager to sell, Gillian found a feather duster and touched a few items round the shop.

The doorbell clanged and the woman came in. After

ten minutes of indecision she bought an antique ring and a cameo pendant. From then on, Gillian did not have a moment to herself. Even as she took her coffee-break, a man came in and looked round, although he left without buying.

When Randall and Everett returned towards the end of the morning, she was wrapping an ornament for a customer, accepting a cheque and smiling her thanks at the woman's retreating figure.

'I've hardly stopped since you left,' she told Everett excitedly, as though the news would persuade him that the tide had turned and they need not sell the business after all.

Everett's smile held a touch of sadness as he looked at her eager face. 'Tell Randall,' he suggested. 'It all belongs to him now.'

Her glance dulled, moving to the new owner. Addressing her fiancé but looking at Randall, she said heavily, 'So events moved faster than you predicted, Everett.'

'Randall was anxious to get the matter settled,' Everett answered resignedly.

'I wanted no nonsense about a change of mind,' Randall told her. 'Persuasion—of the appropriate kind,' his smile was sardonic, 'from the woman you're going to marry, can be potent and effective. Naturally, Everett has a weak spot where you're concerned——'

'You don't know anything,' she flung at him.

'Will you stay on, Miss Taylor?' he asked, with a mocking smile. 'Or will you find it too difficult to transfer your company loyalty from Everett to me?' She did not answer and he went on, 'Assuming, that is, that you possess any loyalty at all?' The raised eyebrows underlined the sarcasm.

Everett, knowing about their past relationship, looked away as if mentally absenting himself. Gillian knew, however, that his very presence acted as a restriction on her freedom to defend herself to Randall about her desertion of him nearly four years ago. Not that she could ever tell him the truth, anyway, she thought sadly.

'Assume what you like.' Her voice was weary, her enthusiasm having forsaken her. There was a brief silence and her eyes were drawn to Randall's face. He was looking at her. His aloof, impersonal gaze tightened the imaginary loop which their reunion—without reconciliation—had slipped around her neck.

'Randall,' Gillian said quietly, 'I have to tell you something. Everett knows—about us, I mean.'

Randall looked quickly at Everett. 'You want to back out of the deal?'

Everett shook his head. 'Gillian told me yesterday, but I still sold the business to you this morning, didn't I?' He turned towards the office, then turned back. 'Right from the start of our engagement I've known there had been a man in her past.'

'He didn't know who,' Gillian interposed, 'until yesterday.' Her smile was strained. 'An amazing coincidence, don't you think? That it should be you who came along in answer to Everett's advertisement, I mean.'

Randall shrugged. 'These coincidences happen to all of us.'

'Come into the office, Randall,' Everett invited.

The office! She should have been more cautious, Gillian chided herself. Saying 'Excuse me,' to Randall, she pushed past him and grasped Everett's arm as he stood by the desk. Randall's jaw moved ominously at her action, but he stayed where he was.

Gillian urged Everett into a corner, went on tiptoe and whispered in his ear, 'The photo—it's in the top drawer. *Please* try and cover it if you get something from there.'

Everett nodded, smiling understandingly. She smiled back, but the smile died as she met Randall's hard look. 'I'm sorry,' she apologised as she passed him more politely this time, 'but I'm sure you share secrets with your fiancée, too.' Then she turned on to him a dazzling, artificial smile.

He inclined his head curtly and closed the office door on her. The men's voices droned on through the rest of the morning. When they emerged Gillian had just turned the 'Closed' sign after the final customer before lunch.

'Gillian?' She turned to Randall, whose face was impassive. No need for surnames or formality now he knew Everett was aware of their past relationship. 'Today, after I've looked over a few houses, I'll be returning to London. Next weekend I'll be back. At the end of this week—Saturday—this place is closing. Over the weekend all its contents will be moved to the new shop.'

'Just like that?' He nodded, his blue eyes cold. 'How do we let the customers know?'

'Use your intelligence,' Randall grated. 'Put a notice in the window, not forgetting to mention our new address.'

'Thanks for acknowledging that I've got intelligence,' Gillian retaliated, her cheeks colouring with anger.

'If you don't like my manner or my methods, you know what you can do. Leave.'

He turned to Everett, who was staring at the floor. Gillian pushed between the two men to gain the sanctuary of the office. Everett moved back politely, while Randall stood his ground. Her shoulder brushed against the solid wall of Randall's chest. If memories rushing back of her cheek resting against its hardness filled her eyes as they involuntarily sought his, it was not for want of endeavouring to suppress them.

Then the implication of his words registered and she challenged, 'You know I can't leave. If I go, Everett goes, too, you said.'

His eyes narrowed. 'I've changed my mind. If you

leave, you can easily be replaced. It's different with Everett; he's an expert on antiques. People like him are hard to find.'

The imaginary loop around her neck closed a little and she pulled at the neck of her dress as if the rope was really there. There was a tightness in her throat at his intractable attitude. Was he actually trying to reduce her to tears?

She glanced at Everett, who still seemed to be attempting to make himself invisible. Couldn't he exert himself for once, she asked herself desperately, enough to put Randall in his place? Then she realised she was being irrational. He might be her fiancé, but nothing could erase the past.

Everett knew, as deep down she knew, that she and Randall were still tearing each other to pieces over their dead love affair. At least, she reasoned, she was. How could she ever forget when she had so lively and loving a reminder of it who hugged her and cried when she had to go?

Whether Randall was troubled by any thoughts of their old intimacy, or whether he was so bitter about her desertion that, come what may, he had decided to make her life a misery, she did not know. If it was the latter, as she suspected, then as his employee, there was nothing she could do but grit her teeth and take everything from him that came her way.

Again she faced him. 'What about my flat? If I left, would it remain my home? Or—or did you have plans to throw me out on the streets?'

His hands found his trouser pockets. 'Don't put ideas into my head. It's a tempting thought.'

Defensively she sought Everett's arm and looped her own through it. 'Do you really think Everett would allow that to happen?'

'Dearest,' Everett patted her hand, 'you're dramatising the situation. Randall would do no such thing, and you know it.' He bent to kiss her cheek. 'So calm down, my love.' Gillian swung to him in surprise. She had never known Everett to speak so affectionately. Was he telling Randall silently, 'She's mine now', or were his words and actions sincere? From his warm expression she judged that there was no doubt about his sincerity.

'The flat is yours whether you quit the job or not,' Randall said tonelessly.

Gillian forced a 'Thanks,' and went to her desk. While Everett and Randall exchanged a few words, she opened the top drawer slowly. The photograph of the smiling boy had been pushed to the back, and she sighed with relief.

'Did you hear, dearest?' Everett asked.

Starting guiltily, she turned.

'I said,' Randall said irritably, 'that before I leave for London, I'll order carpeting for the new apartment, plus furniture, curtains and so on. Delivery and fitting of them will be arranged, too. I shall leave the key with Everett. The people concerned will be told to get the key from him.' Gillian was leaning back against the desk, supported on her hands. Randall's eyes skimmed her neat figure. She moved restlessly as his look seemed insolently and methodically to strip her. She hoped Everett did not notice.

'Do you want to come with me,' Randall queried, 'and make your own choice?'

'It's your apartment you'll be furnishing. It won't ever belong to me. Use your own judgment.'

Randall lifted his shoulders. 'Then don't blame me if you don't like the finished product.'

'I'll be so grateful to have a roof over my head,' she responded tartly, 'I'm sure everything will please me.'

He turned to go, turned back. 'You do remember I'll be occupying the small room as an office?'

'How could I forget?' The tartness had gone, and bitterness had taken its place.

He must have heard because his cold blue eyes

seared her skin like hoar-frost. Then he lifted his hand to Everett, who said, 'The room in my house is yours whenever you want it.'

Randall nodded and smiled his thanks. 'Next week-end, then.' The nod, without the smile, came Gillian's way, then he was gone.

CHAPTER THREE

THE closure notice in the little shop seemed to panic potential buyers into action. It was as if they thought the business was closing down instead of moving. Maybe, Gillian reflected, they had not paused to read the address of the new store, which was just around the corner, really.

At Everett's suggestion, some items had been reduced, but it was not only those which were pounced on. The small furniture van which Everett had acquired was constantly in use that final week. When Friday came Gillian felt tired but pleased. There would not be as much stock as Randall had visualised for the removal firm to take.

Gillian had forced herself to show no interest in the activities of the furnishers and kitchen designers at her new apartment. Part of her longed to race up the side entrance stairs and direct where curtains should be hung, against which wall the small bed she would occupy should go, but pride checked the impulse.

The memory of Randall's look, tainted with contempt, his statement that he had been 'cured' of her, held her back.

Even Everett did not know when Randall would be returning. 'Saturday morning,' he hazarded. 'After all, he has a job to do, hasn't he? He's based in London, apparently, and it's a long drive from there.'

It was reasonable thinking, Gillian decided, and it meant that she could safely visit the place which, from tomorrow onwards, would be her home. Everett gave her the key, saying that the workmen were finished and had left. 'I'd come with you,' he added, 'but I'd better stay here in case Randall comes, although it's unlikely.'

Gillian was secretly pleased that she would be viewing her new home alone. When she married Everett, she would go everywhere with him and he with her, but until then she wanted to keep just a little part of herself as her very own, unshared and private.

The transformed apartment had her gasping. Everything was of the best quality. The bed was not small as she had imagined; it was a double bed and bore the name of a well-known manufacturer. Bed coverings had been piled on to a chair. Curtains and bedspread matched, the colour of the carpet blended with both. A fitted wardrobe had been built in and two of the doors were full-length mirrors.

Quickly she made the bed, then returned to the kitchen. All the people involved must have worked at lightning speed to install so much equipment so fast. In a dream she moved into the main living room, whose large area had daunted her the first time she had seen it.

As Randall had promised, the whole room had been fitted with carpeting. The lounge suite was velvet-covered, the couch a four-seater. Low tables invited glasses to be placed on them, scatter cushions added bright dashes of colour.

She walked round touching and making contact, as if leaving her finger imprints on everything would make it all hers, instead of the property of the man who had once loved her with a desperate passion, but who now seemed to hate her with a savage intensity.

Wandering back to the bedroom, she threw herself on to the springy bed. Tiring of gazing at the newly-painted ceiling, she sat up and removed her shoes, delighting in the sensation of the carpet pile easing softly through her toes. At the dressing-table, with its swivel mirrors, she stopped, seeing a bright-eyed, pink-cheeked young woman smiling at her.

'You look like the girl I used to know.'

The words had come from behind her and her eyes shifted to see Randall leaning, his arm raised against the door frame, staring at the mirrored reflection. A haunting, taunting smile curved his lips.

She turned from the reflection to the substance. 'That's just an illusion. My whole world——' Swiftly she checked herself. She had almost given her secret away. 'The whole world has changed out of recognition since those days.'

When, with amusement, he contradicted her, saying that four years was not even a micro-dot in the life-span of the universe, she did not grow angry at his callousness. He had never been told how her own world had altered since she had disappeared out of his life.

He looked around. 'Is all this illusion?' His teasing manner gave a youthful brilliance to her eyes.

'It's a dream,' she answered excitedly. 'Yet I can feel it, touch it,' she flung herself back on to the bed, 'so it must be reality.'

Slowly he straightened and walked across to sit beside her. Scarcely breathing, she watched as he stretched across her and rested on an elbow, his chin on his hand. He looked her over, his eyes shadowed. She was conscious of the way her jeans had shrunk to her shape, and knew that her vee-necked T-shirt had come adrift from the waistband.

Keenly, deeply, he gazed into her eyes, as if trying to read in them every happening in her life for the past few years. Something puzzled him and he frowned. 'The same, but not the same,' he said, as he had before. 'How many lovers have you had since me?'

Colour flowed in her face, then ebbed. 'That's my business. You had no right to ask.'

He smiled with a touch of malice. 'At least I know I was the first.' His hand came out and widened the gap around her midriff, then it rested there.

The familiar yet half-forgotten touch of him irritated, yet maddened. His hand moved higher and she wanted both to reject and rejoice in the slow, knowledgeable arousal of her by his moulding fingers. What troubled her most of all was that neither her body nor her mind told her to resist, to cry out to him to stop.

Her throat dried, her breath came quickly. She started to talk, but found that it was necessary to moisten her lips before a word would pass them. 'How many women have you had since me?' The question came out huskily and it was sufficient to tell him the effect he was having on her.

His smile was slow and tormenting. 'I've lost count.'

Her fingers curled in fury, fastening round his wrist and jerking his hand away. She stood up, tugging down her T-shirt and pushing it into place. 'I hope you enjoy your fiancée.' A thought struck her. 'I hope you've told her about—about your past.'

'My past?' Randall stood now. 'Oh, you mean with you.' He spoke carelessly, straightening the jacket of the suit he still wore. 'That was so long ago it wasn't worth the telling. After all, you were just one of many.'

'Why, you—you——' Her shoulder hit his chest, but he stood his ground, even when her fists pounded him. Only when she grabbed his tie and pulled did he catch her hands, forcing them behind her and jerking her back with them until she almost lost her balance.

'You little cheat,' he snarled, 'running off when I needed you most, afraid you'd catch what I had, afraid of the future—or, as you thought, lack of it—with a man who, to your knowledge, didn't have long to live.'

'My back,' she moaned, 'let me go, *please*!'

'You loved me, you kept saying. When I died, you'd die, too. Not another man would ever touch you after me.'

'Oh, God, you don't know, Rand, you just don't

know.' She felt she was drifting into a faint. Her head hung back and she could hear the cry of a baby the moment it was born, the feel of its tiny body pressed against her by the midwife, the tears when she thought of how its father would never see it, never know he had a son. She gasped again. 'Please, Rand . . . I think I'm going to faint.'

He eased her upright, moved her to the bed and pushed her head down as far as it would go. At last she moved, and he removed his hand. Her pale face lifted lifelessly to his.

'Are you feeling better?' There was no remorse in his tone, nor softness in his features.

'Yes, thank you.' He nodded and turned to go. 'Rand?' He looked at her. 'Thanks for all this. I appreciate it very much.' She remembered how happy she had been at her first sight of it, the happiness even spilling over to greet him when he arrived. Her throat tightened.

'It's only sensible, as the owner of a business, to make one's employees as comfortable as possible. That way, you get the best out of them.'

A sudden blind fury rose inside her, but she struggled to suppress it. By his smile, it seemed he had seen it and was satisfied.

Gillian tidied herself, using the cosmetics and comb in her handbag. The streets of the town were quiet, although groups of young people waiting for the discothèques to open made the emptiness echo with their laughter.

The emptiness outside seemed to follow her in as she let herself into her flat. Except for the necessities which would carry her over until Sunday, when the downstairs shop would have finally closed and her move to the new apartment would take place, everything was packed.

The packing cases and overflowing boxes looked a

little pathetic as they stood waiting for the strong hands of the removal men to lift them. The shop's contents would be taken by them, too, to be displayed in the new premises.

The two armchairs were still in use, although one was covered with clothes which Gillian herself intended carrying to her new home. She sank down on to the other and tried to collect her wits. Her back still ached from Randall's rough treatment, and her body still throbbed from the remembered touch of him.

Her head continued to ache with the impact of his unjust accusations, and her inability to tell him the truth, through fear of losing her most precious possession—her son.

Too weary of spirit to do anything but get herself to bed, she rang Everett. Randall answered the call, and it dismayed her to discover that even at the sound of his voice her blood flowed faster. Annoyance with herself made her snap,

'Have you taken over Everett's house as well as his business?'

'That's no way to greet your new boss,' he drawled. 'I could fire you for insubordination.'

'Fire me, then!' she retorted, and rang off. Breathing deeply and trying to calm herself, she tried Everett's number again.

'Dearest, what was that all about?' Everett's tone was a little pained, a little anxious.

'Sorry, I didn't mean to worry you, Everett. But that—that man, he should be put in his place. He's trying to provoke me all the time!'

It sounded as if Everett was smiling. 'I think you can take care of yourself where our new employer's concerned.'

The trouble is, Gillian thought sadly, closing her eyes and seeing a laughing, fair-haired boy chasing a large, bouncing ball across a lawn, I can't. If I could, Gary wouldn't exist....

'I just wanted to tell you,' she said, 'that I won't be over tonight.'

'Anything wrong?'

'Just tired, that's all. Will you come over here tomorrow? The shop's been busy all week. The last day might be busier.'

'I'll take charge,' Everett promised, 'while you move your belongings to your new home. That way, there'll be less confusion on Sunday.'

Gillian agreed, relieved to have the responsibility taken from her shoulders. 'Everett, have I told you,' she said in a rush of gratitude, 'how much I—I depend on you? I mean, you're so reliable. You're always there when I want you.' To her horror, she found she was crying.

'I'll never let you down, dearest,' he responded quietly.

Gillian rang off, too choked to speak. She scrubbed at her eyes, then stared through the window at Everett's house. She had to be honest with herself—her outburst was caused by reaction from her encounter with Randall, by a potent mixture of events from the past and the present. And an all-pervading dread of what the future might bring.

Morning brought a lifting of spirits at the thought of the home that awaited her. Eagerly she packed the last of her clothes, ate a quick breakfast, then washed and wrapped the dishes she had used.

Her arms were full of clothes and bulky tote bags as she went carefully down the stairs. She made her way first into the shop. Over the top of the pile she was carrying she could see Everett's head.

'I might as well take a couple of pieces of furniture on top of this lot,' she joked, then dropped everything she was holding. Her side vision had shown her the face of a tall, brown-haired woman. Her arm was linked loosely through Randall's and from her proprietorial air Gillian knew the woman was his fiancée.

'Oh, dear,' the young woman commented, 'I think you need help, don't you?'

The calmness, the poise and the amused, possessive glance she turned on her fiancé revived all the damped-down resentment which Gillian had felt against fate, against life and against Randall himself, ever since the moment she had realised that a tiny being was developing within her about which Randall could never know.

For all those years it was she who had borne the burden and the responsibility of caring for his son. Yet there he was, watching her sardonically, with his fiancée hanging on his arm, thinking the worst of her. How often had she gazed at the small, helpless bundle in her arms and identified this feature and that expression as coming straight from his father, afterwards crying a little because he would never be able to share the pleasure, and the baby, with her?

Everett was already gathering her belongings into a pile and she started to help him, when Randall said, 'Gillian?' She straightened. 'This is June, June Morley. June, Everett's fiancée, Gillian Taylor.'

June's hand came out. 'I've heard about you, Miss Taylor.' The smile was placid. 'From your fiancée, of course.'

'Please call me Gillian.' Their hands met and parted. Gillian had no desire to make contact with the wooman who was to be Randall's wife. 'Conversely,' she went on, the fight in her eyes only slightly muted, 'I haven't heard much about you. Your fiancé,' Randall made a sharp movement, 'has been too busy discussing his purchase of Bushell's Antiques to talk about anything else.'

June appeared unperturbed at this suggestion of her fiancé's neglect. 'Then we're quits,' her hold on Randall's arm tightened affectionately, 'because I haven't spent all my time talking about him.'

Randall's hands slid slowly into his pockets. Gillian's

flashing glance defied the warning in the ominous tightening of his mouth.

Apparently blind to the interplay of tension between her husband-to-be and the jean-clad, tousled-haired blonde girl who had scattered the shop floor with what appeared to her to be articles for the charity jumble sale, June announced, 'My life is full to overflowing, you see. I belong to so many societies, not to mention my work.'

'Miss Morley—I mean June——' surprisingly a faint flush appeared on Everett's cheeks, 'is a computer programmer working in telecommunications. Isn't that right, June?'

'It sounds so terribly clever all the men shy away,' June commented, 'except,' with a half-smile at her fiancé, 'Randall.'

'Do you,' Gillian was by now feeling completely out of her depth, 'do you work for the same company as Randall?'

'No,' Randall answered tersely.

'We met,' June went on, 'through mutual friends. When I introduced him to my mother, she was delighted with him.' She flung Randall a roguish glance. ' "You must have him as your husband," my mother told me. "He's clever, ambitious and all reason".' Another small smile at Randall. 'When I told him what my mother had suggested, he agreed. Now I've told you how we came together, you tell me how you and Everett decided to get married.'

Just like that, Gillian thought. 'We came together.' No emotion, no love, just decision! So Randall was 'all reason', was he? Where was the Randall she had known? Passionate, dark-eyed ... reaching out and growling, 'Where's my woman?'

Randall was watching her every expression, but she did not care. If he could read her thoughts, then she hoped they were giving as much pain to him as they were to her. One thing she could never imagine, she thought with a secret smile, was Randall saying those words to *this* woman!

'So,' she tucked her checked shirt back into the waistband, knowing Randall's eyes were watching her movements, 'your fiancée's mother chose you for her daughter, did she, Randall?' Her eyes sparked at him like dancing fireworks.

Randall caught the light of battle and his own gaze took up the challenge. 'You could say she did,' he cracked back, 'except that I had already—if silently—done the "choosing". I let Mrs Morley think her decision that we should marry was hers, of course.'

He watched the light in Gillian's eyes dull to anger, then he smiled. 'You haven't answered June's question,' he said. 'Was there romance in the air when Everett proposed to you, Gillian? Was the sky lit by the moon and were the stars glittering overhead?'

The starlit, moonlit nights in which they had walked back to his room which she'd shared with him! Yet now he was laughing at those cherished memories of their short, impassioned time together.

Everett answered Randall's question. 'Gillian came to work for me. She just walked into my life.' His fair skin coloured at his out-of-character attempt to romanticise and dramatise an ordinary, unromantic occurrence.

The spark had ignited again as she looked at Randall. 'It didn't take Everett long to decide not to let me walk out of his life. And I had no objections to staying right there. He's solid, dependable and predictable and—and has a loving heart. I've always admired those qualities in a man.' Her stare challenged Randall to contradict.

His eyes were like pieces of sharpened flint. 'Very wise. But then one always admires qualities in others which one doesn't possess oneself.'

Gillian drew in her lips. 'Why, you——' She choked back the rest, coughed with her hand over her mouth and went on, 'You're absolutely right.' But her gaze told him, You're wrong, wrong!

'Just as one always admires the other woman's partner,' June interposed blandly.

Gillian remarked sweetly, 'I think you can speak for yourself, June.' With another snapping look at Randall she added, 'I'm quite satisfied with mine.'

Everett's hand reached out and sought Gillian's. He squeezed her fingers, then released them. He seemed moved and strangely grateful.

June turned, saying, 'This wonderful house the agents have told us about, darling—aren't we going to see it? Eleven o'clock, the man said.' She glanced at her watch. She addressed the others, smiling. 'It seems just the right size for the three of us.'

'Three?' The question came sharply from Gillian. Her heart began to hammer. Oh God, she thought, was there a child expected . . .?

'My mother will be coming to live with us,' June explained coolly. 'You see, I've lived with her since my father died, and I insisted that she should come to us after we're married. Randall didn't mind, did you, darling?'

'Were you on your way to the flat?' Randall asked Gillian, ignoring his fiancée's question.

Gillian bent down to gather the things she had dropped. Everett put the clothes on top of the pile. If Randall's dismissing me, she fumed, he can think again! 'Don't worry about me,' she answered offhandedly. 'I can take care of myself.'

'You can't walk through the streets like a two-legged stall in a market-place,' Randall commented. 'My car's outside, I'll take you round there.'

'If I needed transport, Everett would provide it.' She had the door open and was edging her way through it sideways. She felt herself being propelled firmly to the curb.

A woman stopped to look in the shop window,

which effectively prevented Gillian from arguing with Randall as he lifted the bundle from her. He told her to open the rear door, then threw the bags and clothes on to the back seat.

Walking to the passenger door, he unlocked it and told her to get in. She obeyed, having no other option. 'You'll be late for your appointment,' she said bad-temperedly as Randall turned the corner into the high street.

'That's my concern,' he snapped back.

They shared the belongings between them and climbed the stairs to the apartment. Everything smelt new, the carpets, the curtains, even the air seemed perfumed. When Gillian saw the flowers arranged in a crystal vase on a low table in the living-room, she threw down her bundle of clothes and rushed across to the source of the delicate scent.

'How nice of Everett!' she exclaimed. 'Flowers *and* a vase——' There was a small card placed beside them. It bore two words. 'Welcome. Randall.'

Gillian turned slowly. 'Why?' It was a whisper.

'Has there got to be a deeper reason?'

She looked down, fingering the card. 'I suppose not. It——' She endeavoured to clear the huskiness from her throat. 'It was very kind of you. I appreciate the gesture.'

'Would you have been more pleased if it had been Everett, after all?'

'No—I mean *yes*. Oh, I don't know.' She turned back to the flowers, inhaling the individual scents. These blooms were cultivated, beautiful with their vivid colouring.

Other flowers drifted into her mind, blowing in the breeze, daisies, buttercups, dandelions and clover. All those madly happy, yet desperate months of running through the meadow, ankle-deep in grasses and bright, wild-growing blossoms, making love and laughing, then crying silently because of the inescapable fact that, soon, it would all be over.

One of them would not live, while the other would spend her life barely half alive. Until that day she knew for certain that she carried the other's child. . . .

She turned on him, her eyes brimming. 'Why her, Randall? What has she got that makes you want to marry her?' She looked down at herself, seeing her own inviting curves. 'Where's the shape you used to look for in——' "Me", she'd wanted to say. 'In women? Why June Morley when there were surely so many others you could have married?'

He did not answer, just went on gazing at her, narrow-eyed, thumbs hooked into belt.

'Where's her warmth?' The smile she summoned was weak. 'She must be like a snow-woman when you take her in your arms. She's cold, Randall. Her mother said *you* were all reason. What about her? There's not a milligram of emotion in her body. Is there—is there, Randall!' He watched and waited. 'I just can't imagine anyone more different from me——'

Her breath caught, her eyes grew large and the last of the tears trickled away. 'That's it!' she exclaimed. 'That's it, isn't it? It's because she's so different that you chose her.'

'You think I remember that far back?' His jaw was ridged, his eyes hard.

'Why, you miserable——' She swung to the flowers, gathered them in both her hands to grasp and throw . . . She couldn't do it. Gently she released them, easing them back into the water. Their perfume was heady and she inhaled their sweetness.

'I selected her,' his harsh voice went on, 'because she'll ask nothing of me. We'll make love, of course.'

She faced him, his callousness touching off her sarcasm. 'But of course. In a nice genteel way, you the gallant gentleman and she the simpering, obedient wife.' He was unmoved and she choked. 'When were *you* a gentleman when you took me in your arms, and we—and we——'

Her hands covered her face and for a few moments she could not speak. She whispered, 'Are you going to go on hating me for the rest of our lives?'

'The question, my sweet, is irrelevant, since I won't know you for the rest of your life.'

His footsteps as he left the flat were cushioned by the stair-carpet. But nothing, not even the pillow on the bed, could cushion her hurt as she buried her face in its softness.

'The house is a dream!' June remarked, crossing her legs and adjusting the elegantly draped neckline of her peach-coloured silk dress.

A man in love, Gillian reflected, running her fingers over the carved wooden arms of the antique chair she was occupying, would have shifted his eyes at once and looked with more than interest on the slender legs and ankles which June's movement revealed. Randall's gaze, however, was on the net-curtained windows of Everett's house, where they had dined.

It was Everett who smiled at June, not Randall. It was a host's polite, encouraging curve of the mouth, but, Gillian noted with a small shock, his expression was one of admiration. So the woman had something, she concluded sourly. Two men in the room—one was marrying her, the other, maybe, coveting her? A glance told her that it was perhaps too strong a word. But the appreciation was there. What has she got, Gillian considered, that I haven't?

Stealing a glance at Randall, she saw that his gaze had not shifted. He leant back in his chair, legs thrust out and crossed at the ankles, hands hidden in slacks pockets. Her eyes crept over his shirt, and she recalled the hardness of his chest, the strength of his arms as they used to hold her to him.

His eyes were on her now, repaying the compliment.

There was no smile to soften the hooded look as he appraised the full shape beneath the hugging emerald velvet top with its narrow shoulder straps. He looked at her legs, seeming especially interested in her thighs which the tight pleats of her skirt closely outlined.

'It's a dream,' she heard June repeat, as if from a distance. 'It has everything I want. There's a couple of rooms and a bathroom for Mother, a bedroom for me and one for Randall, so that,' with an arch smile at her fiancé, 'if he has to work late—he often does, you know—he won't disturb me when he comes to bed in the small hours.'

Gillian's look darted incredulously from June to Randall, only to encounter his cynical smile. Didn't it worry her, Gillian wondered unbelievingly, if her husband found solace and relief with other women? Wasn't that what Randall's cynicism implied? If anybody knew about Randall's passionate nature and his physical needs, it was herself . . .

Her eyes sought his and she coloured to find his gaze on her. He was not smiling now. Was he, too, remembering? And was he remembering also how he had felt when he discovered she had gone? He was looking at her in the way that he should be looking at his fiancée, with assessment, speculation and barely-veiled desire.

If Everett was watching—but he, it seemed, was talking to June, about the new house, whether it should be filled with modern or antique furniture, matters she should be discussing with Randall, not a stranger, as Everett was to her.

'June.' Randall stood up. 'The hotel will be locking us out.'

'Darling,' June's head swung round to him, 'your wish is my command.'

There was a twang of repulsion in Gillian's stomach as she heard the sickeningly submissive words. Aloud, she queried, 'So you aren't staying with Everett?'

'I've only got one spare room, dearest. You know that.'

'Does that matter?' Gillian asked, with mock-innocence and wide eyes.

'Randall,' June's voice was brittle and acutely upper class, 'I think it's time you put your employee in her place. In view of what I said, Miss Taylor, about separate bedrooms even after Randall and I are married——'

'Oh, so you did! I do apologise, Miss Morley.' Gillian managed to keep her smile from showing.

'I have yet to decide,' Randall commented cuttingly, 'just where Miss Taylor's place is.'

The threat which was mixed in with the subtle innuendo had Gillian moving in swift defiance to her fiancé's side. Her arm went round him. His immediate response, as she had guessed, was to put his arm round her waist and gently pull her closer.

There was no talking to either of the men next morning. Catching Randall in the few moments in which he allowed himself to swallow coffee, Gillian discovered that June had returned to her home in London.

'It would be a good idea,' he said sharply, 'if you got yourself out of the way, too.'

Her eyes snapped and her teeth, too. 'Your wish is my command, *darling*!' Her defiance withstood his shrivelling glare. 'I'll disappear from your life, just like——' *I did before*. The errant words were restrained just in time. 'Just like your fiancée,' she finished, and turned her back on him.

Everett came into the shop with one of the movers. 'There's nothing you can do to help, Gillian, so I should go and take it easy in your new flat if I were you.'

'That's two of you want to get rid of me.' Everett looked astonished. 'Randall's already told me——' The mover scratched his head, as if hoping the argument would soon stop. 'Everett,' Gillian turned to him, 'do you mind if

I borrow your car to——' The telephone rang in the small office and Gillian pushed her way through the chaos to answer it.

'Mummy?' A small, wavering voice touched her ear and turned to 'fast' the speed of her heartbeats.

'If it's me they want,' Randall called out, 'tell them I'm——'

'Just a moment, darling,' Gillian murmured. She put the phone down, shut the door in Randall's face and ignored his angry, 'Hey, what the——'

'Gary love, I——'

'Mummy, I'm not feeling well. I've got—the doctor says I've got a—a chest and——' there was a spasm of coughing, 'and Mummy, I want to see you!' The voice rose to a wail.

'Gillian?' The telephone had been handed over. 'I'm sorry about that. He pulled my arm down and spoke, so I let him have his say.'

'Eve, is it serious?'

'A bad cold that's gone to his chest. Nothing to worry about, but he's so miserable and he's been asking for you. I thought I'd better let you know.'

Eve Beckett was an old school friend. She had married young and gone with her husband to live in Yorkshire. When their baby was expected, they had been so poor they had not been able to afford a car. The motorbike Jack had bought was the one he had been riding when a lorry, about to overtake him, had skidded on an icy road, and the shock of Jack's death had caused Eve to have a miscarriage.

Some time after Gary was born, Gillian had replied to an advertisement and been accepted by Everett Bushell as his assistant in his shop in the south of the country. Since it would clearly have been impossible for her to take Gary, Eve had offered to foster him. He had taken the place of the child she had lost.

Gillian lowered her voice. 'We're moving shop here,

Eve. I've been told I'm in the way. I'll take a day or two as part of my holiday and come straight away.'

Gillian opened the door of the office. Randall turned. His gaze seemed belligerent. 'What do you want?' he asked.

'Everett. Where——?' Everett came in from the street, his shirt-sleeves rolled up. He caught Gillian's eye and she beckoned. He nodded, telling Randall he wouldn't be a moment. Randall did not look pleased.

Gillian closed the office door and told Everett the news. 'Just a couple of days. You don't mind, do you?'

'Dearest,' he said, running the back of his hand across his forehead, 'you know I don't. But I'm not the one you should be asking. Randall's our employer.'

'He's the last person I can tell—you know that.' Everett shook his head as if he could not work out the answer. 'I'll—I'll tell him something.'

Everett returned to the shop and Gillian followed. Randall watched them, his hand combing back his fair hair, and Gillian confronted him.

'I'd like a couple of days off, please. They can come off my holiday allocation,' she added quickly.

His eyes narrowed suspiciously. 'Why?'

'An—an errand of mercy.' She was treading on dangerous ground. Her tongue moistened her lower lip. 'An old school friend.' That, at least, was true. 'There's illness in the house, and she's alone. Her husband died, you see.'

Everett left the shop, arms loaded.

'For "her", read "he",' Randall said caustically. 'Gary, I think you called him?'

Gillian's eyes closed as the pain of hearing Randall speaking his son's name tortured her. Perspiration started on her forehead, her upper lip. Somehow she had to divert his train of thought, and, moreover, convince him. 'Her name is Eve—Eve Beckett. She lost her husband in tragic circumstances. She needs help, my help.'

Randall's smile was faintly mocking. 'You're a convincing liar—almost. Okay, take your couple of days, but make sure it's no more. Right?'

Gillian was out of the door, waving to Everett and racing to the corner of the street. The new apartment was strewn with her belongings, but in spite of that her suitcase was soon packed. There were clothes at Eve's place for the times she went to visit her.

The taxi she had called hooted outside, and in a short time she was at the station, waiting for the train. The wait, the journey, seemed never-ending. She had forgotten to bring a magazine, but she had her thoughts—thoughts which, she told herself, she did not want to think. Instinct must have told her she had almost arrived, since she woke with a jerk from a deep, troubled sleep.

Half an hour later she was seated beside the bed of her fair-haired, flushed little son. He was gripping her hand with both of his, saying, 'You came because I told you to, didn't you, Mummy?'

Gillian smiled, thinking, He has his father's arrogance as well as his father's deep blue eyes. Then a coughing spasm shook him and he half sat up, reaching out for her. He put his cheek against hers and grew calm again.

Gillian was back in the past, remembering other arms which had reached out, a rougher cheek finding hers, as together they faced the empty future. . . . Not knowing how fate would twist and turn, giving them back the years which they had, at the time, thought it would snatch away.

'The doctor's given him tablets,' Eve told her from the doorway. 'He thought a few more days should clear it. He's over the worst, but fretful.'

'Auntie Eve's been giving me big pills,' Gary said importantly, 'but I've got a big throat,' he opened his small mouth and pointed, 'so they go down quickly.'

'Then you're very clever,' his mother told him, feeling his brow and finding it cool.

'Clever,' Gary repeated, liking the word. 'Is my daddy clever?'

Every time she visited him she had shown him the picture of Randall she had kept in her handbag through the years. She had wanted him to know his father, believing that he would never see him. She checked her thoughts. In spite of the changed circumstances, Gary would still never see him.

'Your—your daddy's clever, very clever,' she assured him, smiling.

Eve caught up with the statement quickly. 'Is?' she queried. 'Past tense, surely? Unless you're referring to Everett?'

Gillian shook her head and Eve's eyes opened wide. 'Have you eaten?' she asked casually. 'No? You must be famished. Come on, I'll get you some food.'

'Don't go,' Gary pleaded. 'Stay here.'

'I'm here for a day or two,' she told him. 'But right now,' she patted herself, 'my tummy's empty.'

Gary laughed and released her hand. At the door, Gillian said quietly to her friend, 'There's a great deal to tell you.'

The telling took all of the mealtime and through washing the dishes. 'Will you tell him about Gary?' Eve asked.

'Don't you see,' Gillian answered, 'it's the last thing I can do. He'd take Gary away from me.'

Eve looked doubtful. 'From your description of his fiancée, it doesn't sound as though she'd be the sort to take kindly to the idea of having Randall's love-child wished on her.'

Gillian let out a sigh. 'That's true. But he's grown so ruthless, Eve, so hard. He'd find some other way, if only to hurt me.' She put down the tea-towel. 'He's changed so much he's like a stranger. I can't see in him the warm, human man he used to be.'

'The one you loved so much?' Gillian nodded. Eve

smiled gently. 'In the circumstances, it's just as well, isn't it? I mean, you've both got marriage partners lined up. Wouldn't it be awful if you found you were still in love with him? Hey, Gillian,' she looked into her companion's pale face, 'you're not, are you? For heaven's sake, what are you going to do about it?'

Gillian smiled wanly. 'Marry Everett, of course.'

Gillian stayed at her friend's house for the full two days which Randall had specified. On the second day, when she had told Gary that she would be leaving, he had cried and clung, so she took the risk and promised him one more day.

'I must phone Everett,' she told her friend that evening, only moments before the telephone rang.

'That could be him,' Eve remarked as she went into the hall. She returned almost at once. 'For you—a man.' She made a face. 'Definitely not Everett.'

Gillian's heart had begun to pound even before she reached the phone. 'Yes? Of course it's me. That was Eve, my friend. Who did you expect, a man?'

'Someone called Gary?' Randall asked silkily. Gillian was too tormented to answer. 'I thought I said two days? We need assistance in the new shop. I'm taking time off from work to take your place. I've discovered I'm not cut out to be a sales assistant.'

'Too bad-tempered with the customers?' she asked sweetly.

'I'll give you till tomorrow,' he replied curtly.

'Mummy,' it was a stage whisper through the banisters from a curled up Gary, seated and straining to listen, 'I want you to stay.' Urgently she shook her head, and Gary's voice rose to a wail. 'I want you to stay!'

Eve ran up the stairs and carried a protesting Gary back to his bedroom.

'Sorry about that,' said Gillian.

'Do you know,' the words came slowly, with curiosity, 'I could swear I heard the word "Mummy".'

'Eve's friend's child,' she lied—closing her eyes and crossing her fingers. 'The—the child's mother isn't well and——'

'You should write stories for children,' he interrupted caustically. 'Your inventions would be swallowed whole—by them.'

'For goodness' sake,' she blurted out, 'why are you so suspicious of everything I say?'

'You're such a bad liar,' he told her blandly.

Gillian kept her fingers crossed, hoping he would not pursue the matter. To her relief, he said, 'Tomorrow morning at nine.'

'I couldn't make it by then, Randall. Yorkshire's a long train journey.'

'So that's where you are. Which part?'

'Well——' Should she tell him? There was little alternative, but she decided to be vague. 'There's York, then a fairly long drive by car or taxi. It's beautiful countryside, Randall. Eve's lucky to live here.'

'Okay, so you're not telling me. Make it tomorrow, the earlier the better.'

The telephone was rammed down.

'Phew!' sighed Eve, standing at the foot of the stairs. 'So that's Gary's——' She covered her mouth and gazed up the stairs, but the landing was empty. She led the way into the living-room. 'My word, he must be difficult to handle! I do see what you mean about not telling him. If he knew, you wouldn't stand a chance. He'd be here like a shot, and you'd be one lovely little son less.'

Gillian felt choked. 'I don't know how he'd stand legally if he did take Gary, but that wouldn't matter to him. He'd—he'd take him away and hide him, and he'd never let me see him again.'

Eve guided her to a seat. 'Don't upset yourself. It won't happen, will it? He'll marry that woman—sorry,

Gillian, you may feel like that about him, but you've got to face facts. He seems to have the path of his life mapped out pretty well. You've got to harden yourself to accept it, but you just don't figure in it, do you?'

A plaintive voice called from upstairs. Gillian was at the door at once. 'I'll go first thing,' she said, 'while he's asleep. Afraid I'll have to leave you to cope with the tears.' She was halfway up the stairs.

'I'm used to it by now,' Eve said resignedly. 'I'll take him out, drive on to the moors, have a picnic.'

'You're so good, Eve, I can't begin to thank you.'

'Don't try. The money you give me comes in very useful. And besides, I kind of love the little feller myself. I'll see no harm comes to him, no harm at all.'

CHAPTER FOUR

GILLIAN carried her suitcase into the shop before going up to her apartment. Everett was serving a customer, pointing out the excellence of workmanship in a pair of eighteenth-century fans. The price was high, Gillian knew, and the sale of the items would assist significantly in getting the business on its feet again.

Not, she thought, that that would help Everett now. Only Randall would benefit from such a transaction. Everett gave her a swift smile of welcome, then returned to concentrate on his customer, while Gillian made her way through to the office behind the shop.

Randall was at the desk, which was placed so as to face the shop. He rose slowly and his gaze, as it slid over her travel-weary figure, was lazy. Despite the half-smile, there was something in his expression which worried her. His tolerant amusement was only skin deep.

'I told you, it was part of my holiday allocation.'

'Was it? Maybe I've decided to let you have the three days——'

'Two and a half.'

He glanced at the grandfather clock ticking solemnly in the corner. 'Three days, as compassionate leave. After all, your *friend* was ill, wasn't he? He needed you.'

The double meaning was plain, as was the sarcasm. 'Yes, *she* did,' Gillian retorted. 'When I've freshened up, where do you want me to work—in the shop or here?'

'In the shop. That will release Everett, who will take my place here. Then I can return to London and my work.'

She picked up her case. 'I'm sorry to have kept you, both from your work and your fiancée.'

Returning through the shop, she made for her own entrance door, unlocking it. To her tired legs, the stairs seemed steep. The case was taken from her and Randall followed her up. At the top, she turned. 'There was no need, but thanks.' She went to take her suitcase, but he motioned her into the bedroom.

He put the case down and straightened. 'I've furnished my office. Like to see?'

Gillian stifled a tired sigh and nodded. Everything a business man could need was there—a desk with two sets of drawers, a swivel chair, filing cabinets, another desk on which stood a typewriter. There were shelves fixed by special brackets to two of the walls.

'Only one thing missing,' she commented. 'A sweet young girl to use the typewriter.'

'I won't need a sweet young girl, will I?' He confronted her, his smile a taunt, his hands on his hips, pushing his jacket back to reveal that strong chest. Did his heart beat more powerfully now than it had four years ago? Then, his arms had held her like bands of steel. What were they like now that he was in full health? She shivered inside as a small fire was lit in her veins.

'Why not?' she returned with commendable airiness. 'Have you learnt to type, in addition to all your other wonderful achievements?'

He walked towards her slowly and the fire burned brighter. 'No, my love, but you have. You may not know it, but you're going to work for me.' His eyes, blue like her own, like Gary's, flashed like the sun glancing off an area of glass.

Gillian closed her eyes against the brilliance, knowing again the liquid feeling in her limbs which no other man had ever engendered within her.

Forcing herself to regain her composure, she retaliated, 'On whose orders?'

'No one's. At my request.' His hands were curving round her arms, slowly, surely, pulling her towards him. 'I've consulted Everett, and he had no objections. "Ask her", he said. So I'm asking you.'

'No, you're not. You're ordering me.' She tried to summon up the will to pull back, but it was a useless effort.

'Overtime payments will be generous,' he said softly. 'When I'm here in the daytime, usual wages.'

'If you think you can persuade me with money——'

'Then I'll persuade you with this.' His hands moved over her shoulders, skimming her throat, cupping her face. When the kiss came, she wanted it, when his mouth covered hers, her lips were already apart. Her hands clung to his hard shoulders. Her body tried to make contact with his, but it seemed he purposely held himself away.

His head lifted at last. 'Tears?' he murmured, using a finger to wipe them away. Of pleasure, she wanted to tell him, of anger at your deliberate elusiveness. 'You'll work for me? Or,' he dwelt on her faintly trembling lips, and his eyes hardened cruelly, 'bearing in mind our past relationship, do I have to go the whole way in order to persuade you? What's a mere kiss to an old hand like you? Running off, although you're an engaged woman, to be at the bedside of a *friend* who's ill——'

'You're slipping,' she flung back. 'Accusation is not persuasion.'

'Okay, you asked for this, and to hell with getting back to London.' His practised fingers had the buttons of her blouse open. For the first time in four years she knew the delight of his arousal, the feel of his stroking hand outlining the enticing shape of her.

She caught her breath as a pinnacle of delight erupted in her mind and took her first steps up it with joy and abandon. Then the steps became hesitant. Everett, she remembered . . . I can't do this to him.

He's so good, so trusting I must not let him down.

'I'll work for you,' she moaned. Randall pulled away from her, his jaw inflexible as she hid her face.

For a few moments there was silence, then his voice cut through it. 'Do up your blouse, pull yourself together, then come down to the shop. You'll see me again in a few days.'

Gillian did not answer. There was simply nothing to say.

It seemed that Randall had been right in his judgment about moving the business into the high street. Custom increased and sometimes there were two or three people waiting to be served.

The weekend passed without a sign of the owner of the shop. Since he had not defined how many 'a few days' were, Gillian did not know when he would come again. Nor did Everett, who shook his head.

'He's buying the house,' he informed her. 'He plans to move his fiancée and her mother in as soon as they can find a suitable tenant for their apartment in London—June and her mother, I mean.'

'They're moving in before Randall and June are married?' Gillian asked.

Everett shrugged. 'It sounds like it.'

'Is he going to live with them until then?' she enquired as casually as she could manage. 'After all, he and his fiancée are presumably adult enough to forget convention and——'

'June isn't like that, I'm quite sure.' Everett seemed genuinely shocked. He spoke so positively, Gillian was puzzled. Then, deciding to tease, she laughed, 'I do believe you and June have had a heart-to-heart about sex before marriage!'

His colour deepened and Gillian had never seen him so embarrassed. For one alarming moment she had a glimpse of what their own marriage might be—lukewarm on his part, affectionate, but found wanting in the basic ingredients of a truly happy married life.

He had never told her why his first wife had divorced him. Left him for another man, was all he had said. Now she began to wonder just why. . . . But she banished such thoughts, repressing also distant memories of shared passion with someone who, in those days, she had desperately loved—and still loved and would go on loving, no matter how long her marriage to Everett might last.

Everett was saying, 'I don't really think you know what you're saying, Gillian.' It was the nearest he had ever come to reprimanding her for her outspokenness about matters which he seemed to think should not be openly discussed. With a sigh, she shook her head, dismissing all the worrying questions which clamoured to be answered.

'Where does Randall live at the moment?'

Everett was cleaning an engraved silver dish, handling it with loving care. 'In a small apartment somewhere off the Embankment. I believe he intends to keep it on. After all, he'll still have his work in London.'

Gillian shook her head, unable to comprehend the very practical, quite unemotional marriage which, it seemed, Randall was going to make. The thought of his becoming the husband of another woman turned her cold. How could she work with him, have him there in a room in her flat, knowing he had probably made love—even if it was unloving love—to another woman?

By then, she pacified herself, she and Everett would be on the brink of marriage, too. That, if nothing else, should prove a large enough barrier to wayward thoughts when she looked at the back of Randall's head, the feel of which she knew so well, or touched his belongings—or thought of the son she had borne him.

While Randall was away, she had put Gary's photograph on the dressing-table in the bedroom. Every morning his smiling, sweet face was the first thing she looked at; every night it was the last thing she gazed upon as she reached to turn out the light.

It was the slow, heavy footsteps on the stairs that brought her to frightened wakefulness. She glanced at her digital alarm clock and saw that it was only six o'clock and fully daylight outside. A door in the apartment was flung open and she realised it was Randall's door, where he had told her he would work.

Her eyes moved and she saw the picture of Gary. She swung out of bed, lunged towards the photograph and thrust it into the first drawer she could find. The door handle was turning and the intruder came in. She was standing with her back to the dressing-table, hands behind her resting on it.

'Waiting for me?' Randall drawled, his drooping eyes heavy, his voice slurred as though he was drunk. 'I've never seen you dressed like that before.' He laughed, head back, uninhibitedly, harshly. 'Of course, in those days,' he said at last, 'we made love under the stars, in the fields, in the woods. The grasses were our nightclothes, the trees our shelter, the turf our bed.'

His tie had been removed, his beard had started growing. As he stood an arm's reach away, Gillian could smell his breath. There was no trace of alcohol, so it was fatigue of the deepest kind that was making him act like this.

A hand on her shoulder pulled her upright to stand in front of him. 'See-through nightdress,' he muttered, his eyes going all over her, 'hides nothing. But even if it did, it wouldn't matter, I know it all, every intimate part of you.'

He curled a hand round her waist and pulled her hips and legs against his own, so that she hung over his arm. 'Are you,' he went on, speaking slowly, 'going to wear this on your wedding night? Do you think Everett will notice how beautiful you are? Will he think of you as a luscious peach which the juice spurts from when you sink your teeth into it?'

Before she knew his intention, he had bent and nipped her shoulder with punishingly sharp, white teeth. A stifled scream came from her throat. 'That will show!' she complained, rubbing hard. 'Teeth marks . . . For heaven's sake, leave me alone! I'm not your plaything any more. Four years is a long time, and I've grown up since then. I—I wouldn't look at you now. I was cured of you, Randall, just as surely as you were cured of me.'

Both his arms were round her. 'I shouldn't say things like that, if I were you. You challenge a man when you're in that state, and I'm in this mood. You could get what you're asking for. Especially when I *know* you so well already. Everett doesn't, does he?' he taunted. 'Ever asked him why his wife walked off?'

'No, and I don't want to know.' She tried to free herself. 'You shouldn't be in here. It's my bedroom——'

'It's my apartment, my furniture, therefore my bed. What's more,' his lips nuzzled her ear, 'you're *my* tenant. Mine, mine.' He was pulling her towards the bed. 'Don't fight me,' he warned. 'If you do, you'll find a stranger. Since you went out of my life I've made love many times, but without a flicker of feeling. My heart wasn't in it—how could it be when it was dead?' He pushed her down, lifting her legs on to the bed.

He lay beside her, tugging her face round. His grip on her chin was painful. 'You killed it—stone dead, and it's stayed that way. No woman can revive it. So if I made love to you, Everett need not worry. It would be through physical need,' he released her chin but caught her protesting mouth with his own, then lifted his head, 'lust, lechery', the kiss came again, 'animal desire.'

The kiss this time bordered on cruelty. His fingers

trailed her neck, then fastened on her arm so bruisingly she whimpered. His hand moved, down, down to her hip, where his hands caressed, knowing her responses, moving and fastening on her thighs.

It was at this point that she came out of the mist in which she had been wandering, going where her sensations had led. With a profound shock she emerged into the daylight of reality. He was taking her over, playing on the feelings he knew she once had for him, not knowing that those feelings still existed, dominating her mind and imprisoning her emotions so completely that she would never love another man as she loved him.

But her love could not change the circumstances, nor unravel the tangled relationships in which they were each involved. Her love had no power to bring his dead love back to life, so that the kisses he had given her had meaning, the desire he so plainly felt motivated by anything other than a man's basic need.

He had rolled from her on to his side and only his gaze touched her now. 'What's wrong?' he taunted. 'Remembered Everett and got cold feet?'

'Cold heart.' Her head on the pillow turned from him and her arms crossed over her breasts, trying to hide from him how they had hardened and filled under his touch. Her throbbing body tormented her. The blood racing through her veins was like liquid fire.

'Oh yeah?' He had lapsed into the language of cynicism, and she knew that he knew just how she felt. 'If I'd carried on, you'd have given. You were clamouring for physical release, just as I am.'

Gillian shuddered, seeking the bedclothes and pulling them up. To speak with such clinical objectivity about the way her whole body had burned for him made her heart go cold indeed. This man was certainly a stranger, but hadn't he warned her?

Randall put his arm across his forehead and closed

his eyes. Slowly his body was forcing him to yield to his fatigue. 'What time is it?' he asked drowsily. She told him and he half sat up, removing his shirt.

He grinned at her wide eyes. 'Don't worry, I won't shed the lot. I'll keep my underpants on. But you know it all, Gillian,' he rested on his elbow, 'every part of me, just as I know every part of you. However,' at last he settled back against the pillow, 'in deference to Everett, we'll keep the final barrier up.' His glance raked her body, first pushing aside the covers. 'Which is more than you did.' He closed his eyes.

She pulled the covers over them both, and was rewarded with a tired grin. 'You'll make him a perfect wife.' A sigh of weariness came from his depths. 'Wife,' he muttered, 'wife,' as though the word both pleased and plagued him. Gillian stayed listening, but the name June never came.

Randall worked in the office of the new shop next day. There seemed to be a lot of paperwork to be done and when she commented on it to Everett, he told her that Randall was making contact with buyers overseas.

'Sellers, too,' he added.

Her heart jumped. 'Does that mean you might have to go abroad instead of just to London?'

'Possibly.' He smiled, touching her hand. 'But I wouldn't be away too long at a time.'

She was about to speak, to ask him whether he had a date in mind for their wedding, when a customer entered. Just as well, she thought. It was hardly the place, nor the time, to ask a man when he was going to marry her.

The customer, a man, was interested in the more expensive items. Everett heard and came forward. When he was present, Gilliant always faded into the background while such transactions took place. Everett, knowing much more about antiques than she did, was by far the better salesman in such cases.

She wandered to the window, rearranging slightly one or two of the pieces of jewellery in the glass-fronted display case. There was a curiously elated feeling about her when she remembered the hour or so she had spent in bed beside Randall. Surprisingly, she had slept again, but only for a while. She had awoken to discover that, somehow, they had come together in the middle of the bed, that his arm was under her, while his other arm rested, in the old possessive way, across her stomach.

Flushing with embarrassment at the thought that, asleep though he was at that moment, when his arms had reached out for her he might well have been conscious of what he was doing, she had wriggled carefully away, hoping not to wake him. But even as she had moved, his hold had tightened and she had been forced to stay where he wanted her.

Later, she had managed to ease away from him, seize her clothes and slip into the bathroom. By the time she had emerged he was up and in the room he called his office. While Gillian had applied her make-up in the bedroom, he had gone into the bathroom, using his own toilet articles and towels he had brought from London.

When she had asked him if he would like breakfast, he had refused and gone out, his eyes as withdrawn as if they were strangers. The two hours sharing the same bed might never have happened.

With a shock she returned to the present. The customer left, looking pleased with his purchase. Everett had promised to have it delivered the following day. As he was going into the office to contact the movers and arrange the delivery, a customer known to Everett came in.

Gillian took the piece of paper bearing the name and address of the buyer of the Victorian cylinder bureau, saying to Everett, 'Shall I do it?' He had smiled his thanks and approached the newcomer, hand outstretched.

Randall looked round irritably as Gillian entered. In a businesslike tone, she said, 'Excuse me, please, but I have to use the telephone.'

The instrument was on the desk, near the back. To reach it, it was necessary for her to lean across Randall and pick up the receiver. He jerked back as though he had been burned, yet she felt the magnetism raying out from him like the sun shining from behind a black cloud.

She punched out the number on the push-button telephone, then straightened, stealing a look at Randall's bent head. He glanced up as though he had felt it, his eyes sardonic on hers. As she waited for the call to be answered, his gaze wandered over her trim figure, from the curve of her hips to the roundness of her breasts.

Knowing her as he did, he could not fail to be aware of how much such a look from him could arouse her. A voice answered the call at last. With an effort of will, Gillian overcame the weakness in her legs and arranged for the collection and delivery of the bureau, saying that it was a delicate piece of furniture and required careful handling.

As she leaned over to replace the receiver, Randall murmured, 'Unlike you.'

Eyes stormy, she was about to reply, then remembered their surroundings. As she turned away, he caught her hand. 'Would you like to see the house I've bought?'

'Shouldn't it be which you and June have bought?'

'It's my house.' His hand still held hers. 'Well?'

'Not particularly, unless——' she turned to look into the shop, 'Everett comes, too.'

'You don't trust me? Not even after this morning?' Her eyes grew wary, afraid that Everett might hear.

'Especially after this morning,' she whispered fiercely.

'Anyone would think I'd raped you!'

'You came near to it.'

He shook his head. 'You were willing. It wouldn't even have been seduction.'

'Will you stop pestering me? I can't fight back. You're my employer.'

His jaw jutted forward, his eyes narrowing. 'In my power.'

He was fooling, as he used to do to make her laugh. She laughed now, and Randall laughed with her. For a few magic seconds, it was as it used to be. The door bell rang as the customer left and Randall released her hand.

'Another good business deal,' said Everett, in the office doorway.

'Fine,' Randall answered, his good mood holding. 'Will you come and view my future home this evening? Gillian won't step foot inside it without you.'

Everett, still buoyed up by two sales in a row, laughed more heartily than Gillian had heard for a long time. His arm went across her shoulders and he placed a kiss on her cheek. To her dismay, Gillian felt the slightest sensation of repulsion, but she kept the smile on her face. Randall looked at her expressionlessly, but she knew his quick perception would not have missed her attempt to feign pleasure.

'We'll come, thanks,' Everett accepted. 'Will you be staying at my place this visit?' Randall nodded. 'You must have risen with the birds to make it down here from London early enough to be at your desk when I arrived.'

'Yes,' Randall replied casually, 'with the night owls. I drove through half-empty roads through the dark hours.'

'No sleep?' Everett asked, concerned.

Gillian held her breath. Would he tell Everett the truth, give away her semi-infidelity?

'Office chairs with a desk to rest your arms and head

on can provide an hour or two of surprisingly refreshing rest,' Randall answered, gathering straying papers into a pile.

Everett laughed and returned to the shop.

Gillian swallowed her panic. 'Thanks,' she managed, relaxing.

Randall's head moved slowly from side to side like an adult reproving a naughty child. 'Hiding your secret assignations from your husband-to-be already?'

'It wasn't an assignation,' Gillian protested, whispering. 'I didn't know you were coming.'

'Nor did I.' He smiled up at her disarmingly. 'I just went where my feet took me. If they led me into your bedroom, can you blame them? They'd done that very thing so often in the past.'

Anxiously she shushed him, finger to lips. Randall shrugged. 'You told me Everett knows about your past.'

'Yours,' she noted silently, not 'our.'

'The past, maybe,' she admitted, 'but not the present.'

He grinned. 'There's nothing in the present for him to know, is there?'

Gillian turned away angrily.

The house was large. It was also beautiful, as June had said. 'Well,' asked Randall, 'do you like it?'

'I like it.' She looked up at the high ceilings, engraved and delicately painted; at the walls, similarly decorated, at the matching carpets which had already been fitted. The room was grand and large, so large it dwarfed the twentieth century human beings who, it seemed to say, had dared to invade its two and a half centuries old ambience. 'Who could dislike it?'

'Oh dear,' Everett exclaimed. 'When I think of my own small house——'

'When you're married,' Randall interrupted, 'where will you live?

Gillian and Everett exchanged glances. Everett

answered. Which was just as well, Gillian thought quickly, since she didn't know herself. 'When the time comes,' he replied stiffly, 'we will discuss the question.'

Gillian turned pink at the amused quirk of Randall's eyebrow. 'In Everett's place, of course,' she stated, holding her fiancé's arm and looking up at him brightly.

His eyes swept the room, the gardens beyond. 'Well, after seeing this, and hearing you say you like it, I'm not so sure.'

'But I like your house, too, Everett. It's small and cosy, and,' her eyes swept to catch Randall's, 'unpretentious.'

His answering gaze was cool and measured. Gillian smiled at him as if she had won a small skirmish.

'So you're willing to live with Everett's antiques at home as well as at work?' There was a veiled sneer in the question.

Gillian did not answer it. Instead she turned to Everett. 'In your talk with Miss Morley, did you and she decide on the kind of furnishing she should have?'

Everett looked uncomfortable, disengaging himself from her. 'When she described the place, I advised antique furniture, especially since her fiancé could afford it. But it is, of course, for them to decide between them.'

'Did you and Miss Morley come to a decision, Randall?' Gillian was prodding him with her spiked smile.

'I think, *Miss Taylor*, that that's my concern. But thanks, Everett, for your guidance. Let me show you the rest of the house.'

June Morley chose to furnish her home with antiques, after all. One afternoon she walked into the shop with Randall, gave Gillian a weak smile, cast a warmer one on Everett, then asked to be shown various items on display.

Gillian retreated into the office at the back. Randall, showing surprisingly little interest in the choice of furniture with which he would have to live for some years to come, joined her there.

Seeing Gillian's raised eyebrows, he answered her silent question, 'I know as much about antiques as I do about diving to the bottom of the sea.'

'But it's your house,' she argued. 'It's your money your future wife is spending.'

June appeared at the door. 'I'd rather go to a London store for the furniture,' she announced. Everett, scarlet-faced with effort, hovered behind. 'It may be more expensive there, but there'll be a wider choice.'

'It will cost you a fortune in delivery charges, Randall,' Everett warned.

'If it pleases the lady,' Randall responded carelessly, 'then she can go to the other side of the world and place an order, and to hell with the cost of delivery.'

June smiled broadly. 'I knew you'd agree. You're a darling, do you know that?' She kissed Randall on the cheek. 'I'll use my credit card, then you can foot the bill when the statement comes. Is that all right, precious?'

'Excellent,' Randall answered, as moved by her endearments as a mountain by a climber clambering up its side. 'Have you finished here? Then let's get you back to your hotel.'

Everett said, as they went to the door, 'Tomorrow I'm attending an Antiques Fair in Central London. If Miss Morley would like to come with me, I could advise her on any items that take her fancy.'

'Now isn't that wonderful!' June exclaimed, seemingly genuinely pleased. She squeezed Randall's arm. 'You don't mind, do you, precious? I mean,' she smiled archly, 'you wouldn't be jealous if I went off with another man for a day?'

'Not at all,' Randall answered calmly. 'It was a good suggestion, Everett.'

'We really must go, darling,' June urged. 'Mother will be wondering what's happened to me.'

Everett escorted her to the door. Randall lingered. 'Gillian,' he said, 'I'm staying for a few days. I've brought some of my own private work. Will you be free after this evening to help me?' Gillian told him she would be. 'Is your shorthand as good as your typing?'

'Better,' she replied, smiling. He nodded and moved to follow the others. '*Precious*,' she taunted softly.

He swung round and saw the tip of her tongue protruding from between her teeth. He thrust a playful fist towards her chin. 'Cheeky witch!' His eyes glittered dangerously. He turned away—to meet the eyes of her fiancé as he stood in the doorway.

For an unguarded moment it was like two male animals wrestling over a female. Who was the victor Gillian was in no position to tell—except that it was Everett's eyes which registered a strange weariness, as though the battle had been long and savage.

Gillian went to Everett's house that evening. She insisted on washing the dishes after the meal, telling him to relax.

He picked up one of the many books he possessed on antiques, some of the books themselves coming into that category. She fussed over him a little, which she knew he loved. She plumped up his cushion, straightened the armchair covers and pushed on his slippers in place of his shoes.

Had she done such a thing to Randall in the past, he would have thrown down whatever he might have been reading and seized her, pulling her on to his knee. He would then have proceeded to silence her shrieks in the way they both knew and loved. Gillian wondered just what had happened to that life-loving young man. It seemed that, with one of life's sad ironies, he had vanished as the promise of cure and survival had grown.

Everett smiled his thanks and groped with his eyes, not for her, but for his place on the page. It was this lack of passionate need for her which she told herself she would have to learn to live with. A nagging worry assailed her as she remembered her faint feeling of recoil when earlier he had kissed her.

To make up for her lack of response and to quieten her conscience, she found two or three of Everett's socks which needed darning, and curled up on the hearthrug at his feet. 'It was good of you,' she remarked after a while, 'to saddle yourself with June Morley's company all day tomorrow.'

He lowered his book. 'Saddle myself? I'll enjoy it, dearest. I find her intelligent and entertaining. She's genuinely interested in learning about antiques.'

'And I'm not?' Injured pride had made her say it. Everett actually seemed to like June Morley! But so did Randall, didn't he? After all, he was going to marry her.

'Don't be foolish, my dear. Are you jealous? You have no need to be.' His hand stroked her hair. For a few seconds her response was tinged with irritation, but in a swift counter-reaction she conquered this, managing to turn a smiling face up to his.

His book was put aside next to her work. He stood up, pulling her to her feet. 'Let me reassure you,' he said, 'how fond I am of you.'

'Fond', she thought, her mind playing with the word while her body responded automatically to his light kisses on her lips, her eyes, her throat. Well, she was fond of him, too; the passionate devotion she had given to another man was behind her now, over for ever. . . . Or was it?

Of course it wasn't, her mind shouted, excited to irritability by—what? Could it have been Everett's hand finding her breasts, stroking gently? There was a sudden animal feeling of wanting to throw him off, put a distance between them.

It frightened her because, she tried to tell her recalcitrant body, this was the man she was going to marry, the man who had agreed, on marriage, to take Gary into the family and treat him as his own. She could not, must not, repel him.

There were footsteps on the stairs. It had to be Randall, since he, like herself, had a key. Gillian tried to pull away, but Everett's arms proved unfamiliarly strong. She freed her mouth sufficiently to be able to say,

'Everett, it's Randall,' but he ignored her warning. It flashed into her mind that he was holding her prisoner deliberately. There was a movement by the door and Gillian panicked, but she was powerless to alter the situation. A throat was cleared loudly and only then did Everett release her.

Face flushed, washed over by an unfounded surge of guilt, she straightened her dress, relieved that Everett, in caressing her, had unfastened no buttons nor sought to penetrate in any way the barrier of her clothes. But judging by the look of censure on the face of the newcomer, Gillian thought angrily, Everett might just as well have been making passionate love to her.

'I didn't expect you back so early,' Everett commented, straightening his tie. Was there the faintest touch of victory in his smile? Gillian wondered.

'June had to help her mother into bed. Her mother has arthritis.'

'I'm sorry to hear that,' Everett commented.

'Then June wanted to watch a television programme I didn't want to see, so I returned here. If I'd known,' with a scorching look at Gillian, 'I'd have watched the television regardless of whether I wanted to or not.'

'There was nothing to know,' Gillian threw back his own words. 'If—if we'd meant business, we'd have gone into——' A glance at Everett's embarrassed face stopped her. 'Found somewhere more private. Anyway, it's time I went home.'

She replaced the needles and scissors she had been using in the workbox and handed Everett the socks she had repaired. He thanked her and she put her arms round his neck, holding up her face for his good-night kiss. If he experienced surprise at the unusual warmth in the gesture, he showed no sign. The warmth of his response surprised her, too.

Was Everett suffering from the jealousy of which he had accused her? Was he not the passive, unconcerned person she had believed him to be?

He said, 'I'll see you to your door, as usual, dearest.'

'It's okay,' Randall interposed. 'I'm taking some papers round to my office at Gillian's place. I'll see her safely home.'

The telephone rang and Everett answered. 'It's June.' He held out the receiver to Randall.

The loud, cloying accents were projected into the room and it was possible to hear the caller say, 'No, darling, not you. It's Everett I want to talk to.' With a shrug, Randall handed over. 'Oh, Everett,' June proclaimed, 'I wanted to arrange a time to call for you tomorrow. Early, I think, since I'll be driving. Oh, yes, did I forget to tell you? You're coming in my car. You see, my mother isn't comfortable in anyone else's.'

'I don't mind, June,' said Everett, so submissively Gillian was annoyed. The sardonic smile which came her way from Randall did not help to restore her composure. 'Yes, outside the shop at nine o'clock. The fair opens just after lunch and carries on until well into the evening. Yes, I'll get a train back, or stay the night somewhere. I'll look forward to seeing you. Did you want a word with Randall? No? Goodbye, then.'

He looked as pleased, Gillian thought grudgingly, as if someone had just given him a golden handshake! She saw that Randall was looking at her as if trying to gauge her reaction to her fiancé's verbal faithlessness, but her face lifted boldly to his, giving nothing away.

A quick analysis of her feelings told her that it was not so much jealousy she was feeling as a repeat of the irritation she had felt once before. How was it that the woman had *two* men on her trail, whereas she herself had—none?

The walk to her apartment over the shop was silent, except for the passing traffic and the conversation of people passing by. All the way there, Gillian brooded about the unpalatable fact that the woman June Morley was apparently able to snap her fingers and get the men trailing after her.

In the living-room, Gillian faced Randall. 'Go on,' she fumed, 'tell me in your usual sarcastic way that even Everett's fallen under your fiancée's magic spell and that I'm about to lose him!'

'I wasn't going to say a word,' Randall answered calmly, 'but now you've mentioned it . . . Didn't it occur to you that he might have been trying to make you jealous?'

'But just before you came in he told me I had no need to be jealous.'

'Which was why he was kissing you?'

'Maybe.' "Let me reassure you," he'd said, "how fond of you I am." *Fond!* she thought again.

'Didn't it also occur to you that he might feel jealous himself?' Gillian shook her head incredulously, but Randall went on, 'He knows about our past relationship. That could be an irritant to his peace of mind where you're concerned. He's also up against another rival, isn't he?'

Gillian looked mystified.

'This person—Gary, whose bedside you went rushing to last week?'

'Gary!' She could not check the laugh that came bubbling out.

Randall was not amused. 'He's male, of course. He's

attractive? Yes. He has enough power over you to tug a few strings and you're off at his command? Am I right?'

'In every way,' she whispered, her eyes large, the amusement wiped from her face. 'He's wonderful, he needs me——'

'Needs you, hell!' He threw aside the pile of papers and seized her shoulders, shaking her unmercifully. 'You two-timing little bitch!' Her fair hair was loosened from its knot and wrapped itself across her face. Her neck started to hurt, her shoulder muscles grew strained. She felt the tears start and he must have seen them, but he did not stop, not until she began to sink, on weakened legs, to the carpet.

Even then he lifted her and she saw his twisted lips. 'You're anybody's, aren't you? If I stripped you now and took you—I know the way, all the way, remember, because I've done it many times before—you wouldn't lift a finger or utter a word to stop me.'

Her white face did not move him. His grip under her arms tightened and he pulled her against him. The feel of him was tantalising, arousing bitter-sweet memories, and torturingly swift responses within her body. Her head flopped to his shoulder. For a moment he allowed it to stay. Then, as if in fury, as if steam spurting from a natural geyser, had shot through the surface of his emotions, he threw her backwards. He rubbed his hands on his hips, as though the feel of her was repulsive to him.

When he walked from the room, after collecting his papers, Gillian sank to the couch and lay back, drained and hopeless. Gary, she thought, remembering Randall's words, he's attractive, like his father; he tugs strings—my heart-strings—and I'm off to his side. He needs me, yes, *unlike* his father . . .

When she aroused herself she saw from her watch that it was getting late, It was her custom to set out her breakfast things the night before. On her way to the kitchen, she noticed that there was light coming from under Randall's office door. So, she thought with a tingle of alarm, he didn't return to Everett's house after all.

Probably, she thought as she slipped into bed, he's sorting through the papers he brought with him. Her sleep was deep, but something disturbed her. Unwillingly she surfaced and listened, only half awake. Imagination, she told herself, and drifted into a state of shallow sleep. An undercurrent of anxiety turned the flow of dream pictures from continuity into jerkiness. For the second time she awoke.

Seeing that it was well into the night, a *frisson* of fear touched the skin of her neck and shoulders. I'm not alone, she thought with a shiver. Getting out of bed, she tiptoed to the door, opened it and listened. Her eyes told her that there was no light in Randall's office now. Her ears picked up the sound of breathing from behind the partially-opened door of the living-room.

Was there an intruder who, having heard her, was crouched, silent except for the intake of breath? She crept to the half-open door and listened again. The breathing seemed regular and untroubled. It was surely that of someone sleeping? A burglar asleep? The thought brought a smile to Gillian's face, for a moment masking the fear.

Gathering her courage, she switched on the landing light, sidled in—and found Randall stretched full-length on the couch. A cushion was under his head, his legs were crossed at the ankles and his arms folded across his chest. Gillian walked across to stare down at him, avoiding the shoes he had removed.

In the light from outside the room she saw that, in repose, the cynicism had left his face, clearing from it the lines engraved by past pain and the determined suppression of it; by illness and its subsequent conquest; by anguish at the deprivation of affection by the one person who had, in all that time of hopeless despair, stood by him—herself.

He must not sleep the night through without a cover over him, she decided, and stole out to a storage cupboard, removing a blanket. This she lowered gently over him. For a minute she thought she had succeeded in not disturbing him. When a deep sigh escaped him, she knew she had.

A hand came out, finding her arm. 'Gillian? My love, my own?' He was dreaming. He thought they were young again and lovers, entwined by an invisible thread until fate tore them apart! It had indeed torn them apart, not by the ending of a life but the creation of a new one . . . Something he would never know.

'Hold me, my own.' His grip was formidable and she did not have the physical strength to resist. Nor did she want to. Her love for him burned as brightly as it ever had before, and the fact that she had given birth to his son brought to it an even greater intensity. She lay down beside him and he moved slightly to give her more space.

Then he pulled her to him. They lay, wrapped in each other's arms, and slept.

By the smiling awareness in his eyes, Gillian judged that Randall had been awake for some time before she stirred. 'Are you part of my dream?' he asked with a touch of mockery.

'Nightmare, probably,' she answered on the same light note. How else, she asked herself, could two people, who were once lovers, treat such a situation except lightly, as if it were of no consequence to waken and find they were still in each other's arms?

'Is this a nightmare, then?' His lips touched hers with teasing tenderness. 'And this?' They trailed her cheek, her chin, finding her earlobe and nipping it, at which she squealed. His laughter was loud and happy, his head moving back and revealing his strong throat.

His shirt was missing and Gillian's hands moved over his shoulder blades, running her fingernails down them. He shouted at her audacity and she answered, 'You shouldn't have nipped my ear.'

'I'll do this instead.' He pulled aside her nightdress and put down a row of burning kisses along her breast.

In vain she tried with her hands to lift his head, fingering the thickness of his fair hair, taking tufts and pulling in her anguish-spiced ecstasy. 'No, Rand, no, you mustn't! There's nothing between us any more. Except two people, one who loves you, and one who loves me.'

Loving, she thought in the swirl of mist around her mind as he ignored her plea and scorched a trail upwards over her other breast. Wasn't that too strong a word? Fond of you, Everett had said. Separate rooms, June had demanded . . .

Randall moved his body on to hers, yet still she whispered, 'No, Rand, no, Rand,' with increasing urgency.

'Yes, Gillian, yes, Gillian,' he mocked. 'I want you, you elusive little cheat. You make a habit of cheating people, don't you?' She grasped his bristle-dark chin and turned his face, seeking his eyes. They were dark and blazing. Why had he turned angry, calling her names again? Dear heaven, she thought, it still rankles, what I did four years ago. Will he never forgive?

'At this moment,' he persisted, 'you're cheating Everett. Look at you—not repulsing me. Welcoming me, instead. No, no,' he stilled her indignant struggles, running his hand over secret, familiar places, 'you're not withdrawing into yourself now. We've gone too far.'

His caresses were arousing her to a pitch where she knew she would be the loser—or would she be the winner? She didn't know any more. It was imperative to stop him before——

'I'm not cheating Everett,' she denied. 'I won't let you take me. It would be disloyal to him to let you make me your lover again.'

'Disloyal!' he rasped, easing from her. 'So what about this Gary? And what about sleeping, *twice*, in my arms in this last day or so?'

'On both occasions it was your fault,' she accused. 'The first time you just got into my bed. This time you pulled me down and wouldn't let me go.'

'And you wanted to go, didn't you!' he sneered, with heavy sarcasm.

Her legs swung to the floor, but he reached out and sank his bruising fingers into her arms. Somehow she pulled free and ran from him into her bedroom. At once he followed, pulling on his shirt and leaving it hanging. His hair had fallen forward and he raked it back. Hands on hips, legs apart, he eyed her abandoned appearance.

'I want to *know* you,' he grated, eyes slitted. 'I want to take you *now*, have my revenge for all the pain you inflicted on me in the past.'

Gillian retreated backwards towards the dressing-table, but he followed. Too late, she remembered. His arm reached out, not for her but for the photograph of the laughing, blue-eyed boy. For a long time he stared at it, face expressionless.

'Well?' he said at last.

'Gary.' She moistened her lips. 'Just Gary.'

CHAPTER FIVE

A CHILDISH voice rang in her head. *My daddy? Is that man my daddy? I want to see my daddy. You can't, darling. He's gone—gone away. I don't care, I want to see him!*

Her frightened eyes, blue as the child's, looked into Randall's. Never had she seen a look in his so savage. 'Whose child?'

Whose child indeed. . . . Yours, she wanted to cry, yours and mine. But if she did, half of her would die, the other half that was left when she had deserted Randall, running from him when she knew about the coming baby.

'Whose child?' Her voice sounded strange. Her tongue ran over cracked lips. 'Why, he's—he's——' She took the plunge, 'He's Everett's, of course.'

'Everett's and yours?'

'No, *no*!' she denied breathlessly. 'Everett's and—and his former wife's.'

He looked again at the picture. 'Curious, curious how——' He flicked her a look. 'You're not lying to me, Gillian?' Unable to trust a word to come from her lips, she shook her head. 'Fair hair, blue eyes, a look of you, I swear.'

Gillian's smile was tremulous. 'His hair is darker than yours. His eyes are grey-blue. You—you're very fair.' She managed a light laugh. 'I'm fair, too. All the world's fair! Of course, Everett's child could—*would* have blue eyes.' He was unconvinced, but as long as he did not guess the truth. . . .

She rushed on, hating the lies she was telling, but knowing it was for Gary's sake. 'The child was born just—just before Everett's divorce came through. His—his wife didn't want him, so Everett got custody.

But he felt a woman—a foster-mother, would be better for the child than himself. Until he's married me, that is.'

'So Everett's such a loving father he farms his child out to someone else to look after? Leaves it to you to rush up to see the child when he's ill?'

Gillian did not, could not, reply. Lies, all lies, she accused herself. But she had to, *had to*! She couldn't lose Gary now, not when Randall was soon to make a loveless marriage, one which, if Randall ever heard the truth and acted vindictively, could make June Morley Gary's mother.

Gillian doubled up at the thought and sank on to the bed, shivering. Agitatedly, she thought, Legally, how do I stand legally? We never married, which makes Gary mine, not Randall's.

It seemed that Randall was waiting for an answer. Would it have to be in the form of more lies? 'Everett was—was waiting until we married, then we'd have Gary living with us.'

'Meanwhile,' was Randall persuaded she was speaking truthfully? 'you keep his photograph beside your bed because you're so longing for children yourself?'

'Yes, yes.' Her eyes looked up brightly and saw the faintest flicker of his eyelids. Had she been too quick to agree with him, arousing the very suspicions she wished to allay? 'I want children, I do want them very much.'

'Pity.' His eyes were hooded as they skimmed her body beneath the semi-transparent nightgown. 'If only I'd known in the old days. The child would be—let me think, about three?'

'Plus a bit,' she agreed with a falsely surprised laugh. 'Gary's three. Isn't that strange?' If her smile grew any wider her cheeks would surely crack under the strain.

'Isn't it just?'

Inwardly she winced at his sarcasm. 'I think he

must—he must take the place of—of any child you and I might have had.'

Randall replaced the picture. 'I think he must, too. Is he,' he strolled acrooss to stand in front of her, so close their legs and knees touched, 'quiet, like his father, or the very opposite as apparently his mother was?'

'Lively, bright, intelligent.' She chose her words with care. 'I didn't know his mother.' She frowned. 'How do you know what she was like?'

'I've discussed her with Everett. He said he had chosen a very different kind of woman for his second wife.' Randall crouched down, resting his hands on her thighs, and an exquisite sensation caught her breath. He must have heard the small gasp as his hands moved slowly, insinuatingly upwards. 'Did he, Gillian? Are you the serious, thoughtful woman he seems to think you are? Passionless, undemanding sexually, putting the intimacy of marriage into a kind of little pillbox, marked, Take rarely, sparingly, never if possible?'

His stroking hands moved higher and she could not breathe for the excitement he was arousing. 'I could have told him,' Randall continued, a half-smile barely curving his lips, 'of the passion-racked lovemaking you took from me and returned in full. I could have talked about the laughing-eyed, bubbling girl with the long fair hair and lovely face that haunted me when she wasn't with me, and enraptured me when she was.'

Now his hands were on her hips, her waist, her breasts. The pain of keeping her hands away from his half-covered shoulders, rubbing her fingerpads in the spread of chest hair, almost equalled the love-pain to which he was lifting her.

'Where's she gone, that girl, Gillian? Did she die when she thought I'd died, too? And am I now like a ghost to you, haunting you, reminding you of good days gone for ever?'

'Let me be,' she pleaded, her voice intense. 'Stop this lovemaking, which you're doing like a—a robot, without any feeling. Because you were cured of me, weren't you? You said so. And I was cured of you, so——' With curled fingers she tore at his hands, throwing them from her, seizing the quilt and rolling it round her shaking body. 'I've got my future planned and you've got yours—all worked out, no doubt, to the final detail. A cold wife, a long line of mistresses——'

He straightened, eyeing her dispassionately. 'And you, frustrated beyond reason, taking a lover; even, who knows, turning to me again, for the satisfaction Everett fails to give you.'

'Think what you like, Rand. Just—just get out of here.' Her voice trembled and he did not move. 'Please,' she whispered, 'just go.'

He went, closing the door behind him.

Gillian dressed feverishly, shivering as though she was ill. Washing, combing her hair, pulling on a jacket, she tore open her door—and stopped at the sight of Randall entering his office.

Afraid he would interrogate her as to her intentions, she dashed to the stairs and ran down them. As she began her race along the high street, she glanced back to see Randall watching her from her living-room window.

It was vital to see Everett before he left his house to come to the shop. Not only would Randall be there, Everett himself would be up and away to London, probably until the following morning.

With shaking hands Gillian found Everett's key, used it and hurried up the stairs. She found him in the kitchen, methodically washing the dishes. He greeted her with a smile and an absentminded kiss on the cheek.

'I thought you'd be having your breakfast,' he commented. 'I'll be coming to the shop——'

'Everett, would you listen? *Please*, Everett, this is urgent. Here, dry your hands. What you haven't done, I'll do later.' She took the towel from him and he waited patiently, hands at his sides. 'Everett, Randall's seen the photograph of Gary.'

He frowned, appearing uncertain as to why it should concern him. 'So you've told him about the child?' he said at last.

'Everett, you know I couldn't. I've told you why.' She was growing impatient at his apparent obtuseness. 'He'd take Gary away from me, and I'd never see him again.' She grasped his arm. 'You've understood before. Why don't you understand now?'

He glanced at his watch, growing agitated. 'I must get to the shop, dearest. June is calling for me. Can we discuss this when I return? If I can't make it back tonight, it will keep till tomorrow, surely?'

'There's something I have to tell you, Everett. I—I lied to Randall. I told him Gary was your child, yours and your ex-wife's.' Everett grew pale and Gillian, unsure of her ground now, stammered, 'I'm s-sorry, Everett, but I just had to tell Randall something to put him off the scent. Everett,' both her hands gripped his arm, 'I know I shouldn't be asking you this, because I know you don't want to be rushed into being tied down for the second time, but you have asked me to marry you, and I am your fiancée.'

Everett nodded, smoothing back his hair with quick movements.

'Well, Everett,' she reached on tiptoe and kissed his mouth, 'do you—do you think we could bring our marriage forward?'

'Is it Leap Year?' The dry voice came from the doorway behind them. The tone had been light, but the look in the eyes was incisive. 'The woman proposing to the man? Tut, tut, that will never do!' He added, with an ironic glint in Gillian's direction, 'Just how permissive can a woman get these days?'

Goaded beyond control, Gillian's voice rose. 'Will you please get out? This happens to be Everett's house, not yours.'

'Nor is it yours.' There was a bitter spite in his gaze. 'Although you're doing your best to get your foot in the door, judging by your request to advance the date of your wedding. You have me wondering, my love, Nine months being the usual time for a——'

'We are not lovers!' Gillian shrieked. She swung to Everett. 'Are we? Tell him!' She shook the arm she was holding.

'We're not lovers, Randall.' Everett spoke slowly, and with a heavy sigh.

Randall's response was to make his way to his room, closing the door. Gillian ran across to shut the living-room door. 'Everett, *please* will you do as I ask?' she whispered. 'Then you could adopt Gary, secretly, of course, and he *would* become your child.'

He ran a hand across his face. He looked as though he wanted to slump into a chair. Instead, he straightened his sagging shoulders and held Gillian's arms. 'You're getting me impossibly involved in your tangled relationship with Randall, my dear. I'll be away for a day. Let's both think about the future—think about it rationally, with common sense and the minimum of emotion.' He turned at the door. 'All I can say is, I wish you hadn't told that lie to Randall. As Gary's father, he has a right to know——'

Frightened of being overheard, she pressed a finger to his lips. 'I'm sorry, Everett, for burdening you with my troubles. You didn't burden me with yours, and I know you had plenty when I first knew you. I didn't want to involve you, or tell those lies, but——' she sighed, 'there just seemed no other way out.'

Gillian followed Everett down the stairs. A door opened upstairs and Randall followed Gillian, who said, over her shoulder, 'What about your breakfast?'

She noted that he had shaved and changed.

'What about yours?' was his swift, revealing answer.

Everett looked from one to the other, then made for the front door. They walked to the corner and joined the high street, three abreast, with Gillian in the centre. The two men talked over her head until a blaring horn attracted their attention.

June had parked at the curb and was waving madly. She got out and caught Randall's arm, tugging him down. 'Just time for a "good morning" kiss,' she said brightly, and put her mouth briefly on his. His arms went round her, but at that precise moment she disengaged from him, brushing her jacket as if she had been embracing a garage mechanic covered with grease.

Everett bent down and was waving to someone in the car. June said, linking her hand in his as though he, too, was engaged to her—a thought at which Gillian smiled, 'Come and meet my mother.'

'Gillian.' Randall was motioning her to join her fiancé at the car door, which was open on to the pavement. Everett had shaken Mrs Morley's hand and she was telling him the front seat was his.

'Who's that pretty young woman behind you, Mr Bushell?'

'Mother,' June answered, 'this is Miss Taylor, Everett's fiancée.'

The slim, grey-haired lady stretched out her hand. 'So formal, June. What's your name, my dear? Gillian? As pretty as you are. I understand you're to be Everett's second wife. Yes,' a considering pause, 'I think he has made a good choice this time, although——' Her doubts were never expressed.

June laughed. 'You and your instant summings-up of character, Mother! You'll be saying next that Randall isn't right for me.' Mrs Morley frowned at the man about whom her daughter was talking, then transferred that frown to her daughter. 'You said he was all reason.' June grasped Randall's arm and looked adoringly up at him. 'Which is how I like my men. No emotion to clutter up the relationship.'

Gillian darted a glance at Randall, whose face as he returned her glance remained impassive. Mrs Morley's keen eyes picked up the flashing interchange, she frowned again, then fidgeted to a more comfortable position in the rear seat. The mother, Gillian decided, had all the quickness of perception the daughter lacked.

'Now,' June was busy organising again, 'Everett, come along in beside me.' She slid into the driver's seat, watching while Gillian held the door for her fiancé. He motioned that she should close it.

'You've forgotten, Everett.' She pointed to her lips. Everett flushed, murmured, 'I'm sorry,' and pulled her down to place a hasty kiss on her cheek.

Mrs Morley cleared her throat. Glancing at her, Gillian caught the tail end of the puzzled frown. The perceptive mind appeared to be working at full power.

As the car slid from the curb Gillian stood beside Randall, waving the passengers off. Then they had gone and Gillian's eyes lifted to clash with Randall's. They were a darker blue now, she mused, than in the past. She could not read the thoughts of this stranger beside her as she had the man she had loved and known—or thought she had known—in those days.

'Let's open the shop,' he said, leading the way.

Alone now, and with thoughts filling her mind of the night's events, followed by the morning's discovery by Randall of Gary's picture, she found herself tense and uneasy, wondering what the next few hours would hold for her.

There was an emptiness in her stomach which she was determined to ignore. She refused to let Randall know how much she had missed her breakfast—but she had reckoned without the rumblings which told him without words of her unindulged appetite.

A hasty glance showed her he was smiling. She grinned back, she could not help it. 'Sorry.'

'Who are you talking to—your boss or your ex-lover?'

She pretended to consider. 'My boss.'

'Right. Your boss says go out and buy some cheese and tomato rolls. Your ex-lover says share them with me.'

'Here, in the shop?'

'We'll lock the shop again and picnic in the shop's office. Okay?'

'Okay. Your wish is my command.' She dodged his playful fist, grabbed her handbag and went out.

They pushed aside the typewriter and papers, spread paper napkins and took great bites into their rolls. While Gillian had been out, Randall had made coffee, using her kitchen and her utensils.

'That's better,' Randall commented, dusting his hands and pouring the coffee.

They drank it in silence. Gillian pretended to be daydreaming, but was conscious all the time of Randall's eyes on her. She wondered whether he was searching for something and if so, what it was. She wondered also if he had believed her story that the smiling boy in the photograph was the son of Everett and his ex-wife. She wished she knew how stable the ground was on which her life was standing.

Gathering the cups and cutlery, she told Randall she was going upstairs to wash them and wouldn't be long. Instead of opening the shop, as she had thought, he followed her up to her kitchen, taking a towel and drying the dishes.

'I've decided to appoint a part-time assistant to help in the shop,' he remarked casually, drying the last cup. 'Any objections?'

She faced him, using the hand-towel. 'I don't know, until I know why, do I?'

'My own private work is growing. The pile of reports awaiting typing is likewise increasing, which means I'll need your help badly. Since you can't do two jobs at once, and Everett's becoming more and more occupied with the purchasing side of the business, I reckoned that if you worked in the shop in the mornings and I got a part-timer in in the afternoon, you'd be free to do my work then. Now—any objections?'

She considered, saying at last, 'You're the boss. What you say goes.'

He closed the gap, reaching out for her wrist. 'Does it? Suppose I said I intend to become your lover again?'

She shook her hand free, colour swamping her cheeks, excitement increasing her heartbeats. 'Don't be stupid!' She did her best to speak matter-of-factly. 'I do happen to be engaged—to another man.'

'You've just told me I'm the boss. Earlier, you stated that my wish was your——'

'I was only imitating June. I should have known better,' she retorted, her colour still high.

His arms linked round her, his mouth touched hers. 'We're so nearly lovers, my sweet one. Twice we've slept together——'

Twisting away, she answered, ' "Slept" is the important word. So is "nearly". We aren't and we haven't.'

'But you are and have with Everett.' His wandering lips felt cool on her throat.

'What are you implying?' she whispered, afraid now.

'That the child called Gary is yours and Everett's.' She ducked out of his arms and backed away. 'And that you've let him be fostered because Everett, in his straitlaced way, doesn't want the responsibility laid at his door—not until you're married anyway. How long has he been divorced?'

'I thought I told you. Two years.'

'And the child is three?' She nodded, her speech deserting her. How long would it take his quick brain to reach the truth? But it seemed he had miscalculated this time. 'Which means the child was conceived while he was still officially married to his ex-wife.'

Gillian closed her eyes to hide her relief. Her answer just had to be neutral. 'Think what you like,' she said finally.

'I will, my love, I will,' was his enigmatic remark.

'I think I know where to find someone who'd help in the shop, without having to advertise.'

He stopped on the way to the door. 'Who?'

'A woman called Isobel Poole. She worked in the other shop at the time that Everett bought it. Everett gave her the option of staying on, but she said her mother was ailing and needed her attention full-time. Her mother died some time ago and I did hear she was looking for a part-time job.'

'Fine. Presumably she has a basic knowledge of antiques?'

'Actually, she knows more than I do.'

'Better still. Which means she wouldn't have to keep running upstairs to you asking questions while you work on my stuff. Right?'

'Right. Your work would have my undivided attention.' She grinned. 'And all for no extra pay, because you'd be paying me anyway as one of your employees in your antiques business.'

'Right again.' He advanced on her. 'And employees who are cheeky to their superiors could find themselves in trouble. This employee in particular, since I already know the ins and outs of her so well.'

His hands followed the line of her figure, pressing against her breasts, her hips, her thighs, where they lingered momentarily. Caught by the hypnotism of his eyes, her own hands moved to place themselves over his.

'What are you after?' he asked quietly. Then she

was pulled against him, his mouth savaging hers, and she was clinging as she used to do, unconsciously endeavouring to hold him back from the grasping inevitability of the fate which, at that time, she thought awaited him.

It was different now. He prised her hands from his shoulders and placed her an arm's distance from him. 'You're four years too late,' he said bitingly, and left her.

After such a crushing dismissal, Gillian felt too humiliated to face him immediately. Checking Isobel Poole's number, she called her. The woman's surprise was instant. 'How nice to hear from you again, Gillian,' Isobel said. 'How's Everett? Are you two married yet?'

'Still engaged,' Gillian answered. 'We've been so busy with the shop. I suppose you don't know Everett had an offer for it and he sold out to someone else?'

Isobel was at once both sympathetic and regretful. 'Does that mean you're both out of a job—no money coming in?'

'Nothing as disastrous as that,' Gillian reassured her, and told her about Randall, about moving shop and the increasing custom gained by the move. 'Randall West and I, we—we knew each other a few years ago, then we lost touch. He saw Everett's advertisement in a magazine, offering the business for sale. Randall was looking for a business like ours to invest in, and—well, I've told you the rest.'

'Sheer coincidence?' Isobel commented, intrigued. 'I've heard such things do happen.' She waited for Gillian to make the next move.

'I was wondering, Isobel, if you had any spare time these days. Randall said this morning that we could do with extra help——'

'Just what I've been waiting for!' Isobel exclaimed. 'I'm right in my guess, aren't I? You were going to offer me that job? Fine. I accept.'

They both laughed. 'When can you start?' Gillian asked.

'Tomorrow? Good. What time do you want me there?'

'Mind if I check with Randall?' Gillian ran down the stairs and found him in the office. 'Isobel can start tomorrow. What hours shall I tell her?'

'One o'clock to five. That way, she can cover the lunch hour and we won't lose any business by closing.'

'Usual rate of pay?' He nodded and she sped up the stairs.

Gillian was ironing a few items in the kitchen that evening when the key turned in the lock. There were only two people besides herself who possessed a key to her entrance door—Randall and Everett.

Since Everett was away in London, by elimination it could only be Randall. She decided to allow matters to take their own course, except that she seemed to have no control over the coursing of the blood through her veins, nor the fast pumping of her heart. How would Randall greet her?

'Gillian?' It was Everett. When her astonishment had receded, she was conscious of a niggle of disappointment, but this she firmly suppressed.

She found him in the living-room, lying back in an armchair. A hand was over his eyes, his face looked pale. Gillian was at once concerned, and she went over to him, wondering what to do.

'It's all right, my dear,' Everett reassured her. 'I'm not ill, just totally exhausted.'

'After a day at an Antiques Fair? It's never done this to you before.'

'I've never spent a day with June Morley before. The woman's nearly driven me mad!' He looked round quickly. 'Is Randall in his office?' She told him 'no'. He looked relieved. 'When he marries her, I wonder if he'll know what's hit him.' He covered his eyes, as if the memory hurt. 'Chatter, chatter, non-stop idiocies, questions you'd expect from a child, not an adult. Yet she wanted me to advise her about furnishing her new house——'

'*Her* new house!' Gillian interrupted indignantly.

Everett shrugged. 'There's only one person in her world—herself. Her mother is an angel beside her.'

'Would you like coffee?'

Everett nodded, but continued before she could go into the kitchen, 'I think it's a case of her clinging to her mother, not the other way round. Her mother has arthritis, admittedly, but her daughter tries to make her think that without her, she couldn't manage. Yet Mrs Morley, I'm convinced, is perfectly capable of looking after herself, with an hour or two of daily help.' He sat up. 'Do you know, Mrs Morley told me that she doesn't really want to live with June and Randall after their marriage, but June is insisting. Mrs Morley wants to stay where she is, in London, but who'll win in the end is anybody's guess.' He looked up. 'Does Randall know what he's doing in marrying the woman?'

Gillian had never known Everett so exasperated as he was now. 'I think Randall knows,' Gillian answered slowly. 'He's no fool. He—he told me he knew it would be a loveless marriage, but that was what he wanted.' After a small pause, she added, 'He said he wanted nothing more to do with love and emotional involvement.'

Everett frowned and examined his linked hands. 'I see. I'm sorry, I believe I've trodden on sacred ground.'

'Everett,' Gillian said agitatedly, 'would I be marrying you if I still hankered after a renewal of my old relationship with Randall?' Even as she asked the question, she knew the answer. She also knew that Everett knew it, too. This time she made it to the kitchen.

When she returned, carrying the coffee, Everett murmured, staring at nothing, 'She reminds me of my ex-wife.'

Silently they drank. When they had finished, Everett stood up and pulled Gillian to join him. 'Dearest, you asked me if we could fix a date for our wedding. Shall we make it a month from now?'

Gillian heard Randall enter the shop. It was an hour before opening time and she wondered if he would come into her apartment and go to his office.

When he did not come, she bathed and dressed and used make-up to hide the shadows under her eyes. It had taken her hours to get to sleep. All night there had been a battle inside her head. It had been a fight to the finish—the finish of her secret dream that one day soon Randall would declare his undying love for her and ask her to marry him. Then she would tell him about Gary. Now she had to face the fact that day dreams were one thing, harsh reality another. There could be no fairytale ending for her.

A month from now she would be Everett's wife, and soon after that, no doubt, June Morley would marry Randall. Gary would come to live with herself and his stepfather, which would reinforce Randall's apparent belief that Gary was hers and Everett's anyway. Just as long as she could keep Gary with her, thus losing the fear that haunted her day and night of having him taken from her, she didn't care what Randall thought about Gary's parentage. At least, that was what she told herself as she went down to the shop to confront Randall.

He greeted her news stonily, his blue eyes cold, his response emotionless. 'A month from now? It's not possible.' He took an envelope from a pile, extracted its contents and thrust a large silver-edged invitation in front of her. 'There's an Antiques Convention in

New York in four weeks' time. It lasts two weeks and it's preceded by a three-day auction of important antique items from many parts of the world. I want Everett to go.'

Gillian was convinced that this was a ruse on his part to make certain the wedding was postponed. 'You don't understand,' she said as calmly as she could manage, 'the articles on sale will be enormously expensive. Way out of the price range of this business and even our ability to buy.'

'I understand perfectly well,' he answered evenly. 'I have in mind a development into the higher-priced market of West Antiques which I'm prepared to discuss with Everett, not you.'

She threw the invitation on to the desk. 'Thanks very much! I appreciate your belief in my powers of reasoning and my business acumen.'

'Neither your reasoning ability nor your shrewdness are involved. You yourself told me that Isobel Poole's knowledge of antiques was greater than yours.'

It was impossible to argue with that statement. 'So we'll have to postpone our wedding.'

Gillian swore that for a few seconds his lip curled with spite. 'You'll have to postpone your wedding.'

'Now I'll tell you something,' she hit back. 'Everett came back from London last night. He was exhausted, not by the work but by your wonderful fiancée. She almost drove him mad. He said she's the most empty-headed, self-orientated, self-opinionated female he's ever met. She's——'

'Don't you think you should let him tell me himself? Stop using June as a weapon to get back at me, Gillian. If there's any revenge to be exacted, I think I should be the one to take it *from you.*'

Turning away, she compressed her trembling lips. She heard a voice in her head. *Where's my daddy? He's gone away. Will he ever come back? No, Gary, never.* Whose loss was greatest—hers, Gary's? Or Randall's?

'I'm sorry,' she whispered.

There was a movement and Randall was facing her. His fingers raised her chin. 'Look at me. What was ever between us is over. You must accept that. Like you, I'm engaged. There are faults in both our future partners. I can see Everett's, you can see June's. *I* can see June's, too. But I don't care, do you understand? She will be my wife, not just in name, as I told you. I'm no monk, no celibate. But I repeat, I shall kiss her and touch her without any feelings *whatsoever*. Whether you eventually learn to love Everett is something I'll never know, never want to know.'

Gillian jerked her chin away and ran upstairs. The thought of breakfast did not appeal, but a cup of coffee was an absolute necessity.

Everett and Isobel Poole arrived together. Isobel had gone by mistake to the old shop and Everett had seen her looking at the empty premises in puzzlement.

'He knocked on his window,' Isobel said, laughing, 'and made wild gestures, which I took to mean "wait for me".'

'I explained that we'd moved and Isobel then said she remembered that you'd told her but had forgotten, in the excitement of being offered a job she knew so well. So,' he heaved a strangely relieved sigh, 'here she is.'

Isobel gripped Gillian's hand. 'It's good to be back.' She looked around. 'Mm, a big improvement—more space, more goods on display.'

'Glad you approve.' Randall was standing in the office doorway. 'In case you haven't guessed, I'm the new owner.'

'Yes,' Isobel commented, smiling widely, 'you've got the look of a successful businessman about you.'

'Ah, no "businessman", please. My brain is strictly science-based. I've bought this a) as an investment, and b) to help a friend out of a basic difficulty—lack of cash flow. I believe that's the current jargon?'

'Well, you certainly talk like a scientist,' Isobel remarked, her long, serious face creasing with her usual happy smile. 'It's great to meet you.' She eyed him admiringly. 'I—er—guess a good-looking man like you is too good to have escaped a female's clutches?' Her open, honest face and candid eyes enabled her to utter phrases which other more retiring people would hardly get away with.

'You're too right, Miss Poole. I'm an engaged man. But I'll always keep a corner in my heart just for you.'

Isobel laughed delightedly, joining in with the others. She looked at Everett. 'You, too. I thought you at least would either be married by now to your beloved,' she indicated Gillian, 'or have kept yourself heartwhole for me. After all, I'm only thirty. I haven't yet given up hope.'

Again there was laughter. Everett answered, with a glance at Gillian, 'We were planning on marrying in a month, but something's come along to postpone it.'

Everett had not seen Gillian since the evening before, having spent the whole morning in his own house with Randall. No doubt he'd been discussing Randall's wonderful plans for the future, Gillian thought acidly. She supposed he was upset by the enforced postponement of the wedding, but she considered with a touch of hurt pride, he didn't exactly show it.

Isobel looked at Everett. 'I believe my hours are one to five, Everett. Or,' moving her glance, 'is it you I should be asking, Mr West?'

'Me. And make it Randall.' His eyes rested sardonically on Gillian. 'Let's be one big happy family. And yes, one to five, to cover the lunch break. I understand from Gillian that your knowledge of the antique trade is good?'

'Thanks.' She sent Gillian a smile. 'Yes, it's good. Not brilliant, but sufficient to judge the value of an item even though it may be brought in with—well, bruises, if you know what I mean.'

'That's fine. You're quite a find, Miss Poole.'

Her eyelids fluttered exaggeratedly. 'Please make it Isobel.'

Randall laughed with the others, glanced at his watch and said, 'Coming, Everett? The Royal Huntsman as usual? They do a good meal there, along with the drinks.'

Gillian watched Everett follow Randall to the door. 'Hey, what about me?' she demanded.

Everett looked back apologetically. 'Sorry, dearest. I'm so accustomed to leaving you behind to look after the shop, I forgot you.'

Randall's cynical eyebrow lifted. Isobel laughed. 'Men!' she exclaimed. 'They're always forgetting women exist.'

'Where men are concerned, Isobel, women can do their share in that respect, too,' Randall commented.

For a few seconds his eyes grazed Gillian's figure, then he led the way into the street, leaving Gillian to close the door and follow.

Over lunch, the two men talked as if she was not there. Randall sat beside her, while Everett occupied a chair around the other side of the circular table. At first, Gillian was content to gaze around her, eating her salad and watching others, listening to snatches of their conversation. Farmers and neatly-suited businessmen from the town's offices laughed together and exchanged jokes.

The low wooden beams and coloured lanterns around the walls brought to mind the many decades, adding up to nearly three centuries, which the building had seen come and go.

Gillian reflected that no doubt the jokes were bawdier then, and that local inhabitants mixed with farmers and labourers rather than the country gentlemen who, in those days, would have taken the place of today's men of business.

When a woman's laughter lifted over the general hubbub of clatter and chatter, Gillian turned to the source of the sound. The woman was the centre of attention of the men grouped around her. The sight made her feel distinctly out in the cold. Neither Everett nor Randall had addressed more than three words to her since they had entered the bar.

She reached across and tapped Everett's hand as it held the handle of his beer glass. He looked at her, taking a swallow of beer as he did so. Randall rested against the banquette, stretching his arm along the ledge at the back of them. Gillian felt its pressure as she leaned back from attracting Everett's attention.

'Did Randall tell you, Everett, why he wanted extra help in the shop?' She gave him no time to respond. 'He wants me to work for him privately in the afternoons. His *own* work, I mean.' She tried to ease away from the touch of Randall's arm which was now in contact with her neck. However, the effort of sitting stiffly upright was too much and she slumped back. 'Do you mind, Everett? I mean,' she knew she was about to tread dangerous ground, but did not care, 'I should really be working in the shop. That's what you employed me for——'

Everett shook his head. 'I don't employ you any more, do I, dearest? If Randall wants you to work on his private business during shop hours, then you must.' His smile was watered-down. 'Whether I mind or not isn't taken into consideration, is it?' He appeared to avoid Randall's eyes. 'Anyway, Isobel will be working in the shop when you're busy elsewhere.'

Gillian nodded, then, unable any longer to stand the pressure of Randall's arm against her neck, she moved round the table to occupy the chair next to Everett's.

Linking her arm in his, she stared at Randall, daring him to comment. He did, not with his lips, but with his eyes. You might pretend you can't stand the touch of me, they were saying, but you can't deny that it has a profound effect on you. Whether touching her had any effect on him, she was unable to tell.

On their return to the shop Everett lingered, talking to Isobel. Her warmth and good nature seemed to flow, as she talked, to her listener, whoever that person might be. It flowed now to Everett, who spoke with a surprising animation.

It was possible, Gillian mused, to forget Isobel's unstyled hair and plain-featured face, and lose yourself in that warmth and openheartedness. Her personality was one that reached out, giving, demanding nothing in return, leaving others reinvigorated instead of drained. Gillian wished with all her heart that her own personality was like Isobel's.

'Everett's asked me to join you for a coffee and a chat this evening,' Isobel said to Gillian. 'Hope you don't mind.' To Randall, 'He tells me you're staying with him while you're here.'

'Randall will make a foursome, I hope,' said Everett, eyebrows lifted in question.

'Thanks,' Randall replied. 'Gillian, there's a lot of work waiting.'

Isobel grinned. 'Her boss's voice! He's telling you to get into that typist's chair—wherever it is—fast.'

'It's in Gillian's apartment,' Randall supplied, a spark of malice in his eyes.

'Everett,' Isobel swung round, 'do you think you should allow this?'

Everett laughed with her, but his face sobered surprisingly quickly. His words, however, were bland. 'I can trust my fiancée. We're marrying as soon as we can arrange another date. The first one we thought of has been overtaken by circumstances.'

Isobel made a face. 'Hard luck. But what's a couple of weeks or so between fiancés?' Again, laughter followed her words.

Upstairs, Randall asked, leafing through papers on a

table near the desk, 'Have you fixed another wedding date?'

'We haven't had time to discuss it, have we, since Everett only knew this morning. But, if I have any say in the matter, which I will, I can tell you it won't be long.'

Gillian heard the odd note of defiance in her own voice. Randall could not have missed it, but he continued without a moment's hesitation, to turn the pages.'

'I hope you can still understand my handwriting,' he remarked.

'I didn't have any difficulty in the old days.'

The pages stopped turning but he did not straighten. 'Yes, you could read it then. Those notes——'

'Love letters, Rand.' She wished her voice had not softened.

'Notes.' He was staring into the past. 'I pushed them into the bushes which bordered the pavement by your father's front garden. It was the only way we could arrange meetings.' Still without looking at her, he continued tonelessly, 'I never did find out why your father disliked me so much.'

Gillian sank into the typist's chair. 'I guess at some time I told my brother Martin about the state of your—health. He promised not to tell anyone, but my father must have got it out of him.'

'Your mother?'

'Did whatever my father told her to do, although it nearly killed her. I know she loved me—loves me,' she corrected herself.

Yes, she knew that all right. She recalled how delighted her mother was to hear about the baby's safe arrival into the world; wrote secretly asking her for photographs as Gary grew and developed; how she longed to see him, she had said, and hold him in her arms. Then, one day, she found her way north to the village in which Gillian was living, sharing a cottage with an elderly couple.

Gillian swung the chair towards the desk, covering her eyes as the tears started at the remembrance of her mother boasting proudly to the couple that this was her grandchild, and wasn't he beautiful, and how wonderful it was just to hold him and kiss him and watch him splashing in the bathtub.

'Gillian?'

Scrubbing with her fingers at the wetness on her cheeks, she jerked her brain back to the present. 'Sorry, I was dreaming.'

His cool eyes noted the damp cheeks. 'Of lost love?'

His near-scientific detachment irritated. 'I'd never waste my time doing that,' she retorted.

The cool gaze warmed with an answering anger, but it remained unexpressed. Randall put the handwritten pages into order and explained that he had printed all the technical terms extra clearly. 'If you need any help, you know where to find me.'

Gillian nodded, flicking through the report, secretly aghast at its length. Looking up at him, she asked, 'If I'm not finished by the end of the afternoon, what then?'

'I'd pay you well for overtime.'

'I wasn't even thinking of money,' she retorted. 'I'm talking about spare time, not overtime.'

'I'd like that report as soon as possible, Gillian,' he replied quietly. 'You'd have my gratitude. Or do you reject that along with my money?'

She saw the irony in his smile, then sighed. 'I can only do my best.'

'Thanks.'

'That's okay.' Her voice had become brittle. 'I always was a fool where you were concerned.' Her prodding words had followed him to the door.

'I told you,' he answered harshly, 'let the past rest in peace.'

I wish I could, she thought, alone again, I only

wish I could. But she knew what Randall would never know—the past would remain with her, walking beside her, holding her hand, and her heart, for the rest of her life.

CHAPTER SIX

IT was almost closing time when Gillian used the internal telephone which had been installed and rang down to Everett in the office. The receiver was picked up quickly and Isobel's voice said, 'I made it. Just before Everett. Gillian? Hi. You want your fiancé, I suppose?'

'Well, Randall, really. Is he around?'

'Nowhere to be seen. A woman breezed in about an hour ago, announced herself as Miss Morley, Mr West's wife-to-be, and demanded to see him. He and Everett had their heads together in here, and I knew they were discussing something important, because they told me. But the woman wouldn't be put off, so Randall came at her call.' Isobel laughed. 'Well, if you could call, "What the hell are you doing here?" as coming at her call.'

'Do you happen to know where he is, Isobel?'

'Well, he did say he'd be incommunicado, but I'll ask Everett.'

'Gillian?' Everett answered. 'Randall's with June at the house he's bought.'

'Everett, do you know his telephone number? I'd like to have a word with him.'

'Well, he did say he was not to be disturbed, unless you came across a technical term you couldn't understand. Other than that, it would have to wait, I'm afraid.'

Gillian gave an angry sigh. 'I do happen to be doing him a favour——' Or am I? she thought. I've done all this in working hours—so far. 'I'm nowhere near finished, Everett. I suppose I'll just have to carry on. This evening—I'll be a bit late at your place.'

'Don't worry, my dear. Come when you can. If it's a

threesome at first, it won't matter——'

'It won't be, will it?' she interrupted. 'Randall will bring June and——'

There was a faint groan. 'It hadn't even occurred to me.'

There was laughter and a voice seemed to come from over Everett's shoulder. 'I swear he's considering calling this evening's get-together off, Gillian,' said Isobel. 'He's already told me what he thinks of the wonderful Miss Morley. But that doesn't solve your problem, does it?'

'That's okay,' Gillian answered resignedly. 'I'll work on, for a while, at least.'

As she typed, Randall's instructions to Everett danced with her fingers over the keys. *Not to be disturbed. Incommunicado....* What were they doing that was so important? Pictures flashed between her eyes and the words she was typing. *I'll make love to her*, Randall had said, *but it won't mean anything*. The very thought of Randall touching another woman as he used to touch her made her feel ill.

Food, she thought, standing unsteadily, I'm getting lightheaded with hunger.

She could, however, find little enthusiasm for the meal she cooked herself, visualising Randall taking June to dine with candlelight and wine. It was, she recognised, jealousy stark and unrestrained, but she knew it was something she would have to live with until—until Everett supplanted Randall West in her affections. And that, she thought, clearing away, would be never.

Nearly two hours later her fingers stopped of their own accord, lifting from the machine and resting lifelessly on her lap. Why, she wondered wearily, am I doing this? For love, something whispered in her ear, and she could not deny it.

The walk along the town's main street was quiet. With a heavy heart she realised that no one had called her on the phone to ask how she was progressing, and couldn't she stop now and come and join the party? Well, she was joining it, whether they wanted her or not.

Using the key Everett had given her, she walked into his house and was greeted by the sound of laughter. Entering the living-room, seeing four people looking at her with surprise, she judged a little acidly that they wouldn't have missed her had she decided to continue typing all night.

Everett was on his feet at once. Randall rose more slowly, having first been compelled to disengage his arm from around June's waist. Gillian was sickened by the sight, by June's dog-with-the-juicy-bone smile, by the remembrance of Randall's words, *I'm no monk.* Had her assumption been right, after all? Had Randall issued the 'Do not disturb' message because he had unexpectedly experienced an insistent desire for the female of the species?

His smile broadened as he watched her hand being taken by Everett. It was as though Randall had acquired his own system of radar and intercepted her thoughts as they zoomed through her head. He had guessed what she was thinking!

'Dearest, you look tired to the eyebrows. Here, sit by me. Isobel will make room for you here on the couch.'

'I'll more than make room,' Isobel said obligingly. 'I'll remove myself to a chair. There,' her smile was mischievous, 'you've got the whole couch to sprawl on if you want.'

Gillian's smile was embarrassed, while Everett coloured. Randall, having resumed his seat, but not his hold on June, watched them both with amused interest. I wish, Gillian thought, as she settled beside Everett, I could read Randall's mind as he seems to be able to read mine.

'A glass of sherry, Gillian?' Everett asked. When she

shook her head, he offered refills to his guests. June refused, but Randall and Isobel accepted.

Randall's arm was round June's waist again. June seemed to have taken the initiative and put it there. Everett's arm, however, had sought out neither Gillian's waist nor her hand. For a couple to be married in a few weeks' time, Gillian reflected, we look surprisingly like strangers who had only just met. Which, she concluded with annoyance, was probably why Randall was smiling, leaning back as he was, eyes half-closed and watchful.

'Randall and June have been busy this afternoon,' said Isobel, breaking the silence.

Gillian's heart jerked and she tensed at what might be coming.

'We've been looking through furniture catalogues,' June filled in. To Everett, she said, 'I decided after all to abandon the idea of furnishing with antiques. I've suddenly gone all modern.'

June's laugh was high-pitched and girlish. *Girlish?* Gillian thought wonderingly. June had left twenty-six behind. Her fiancé was, as she herself knew by experience, a passionate man. Had they not—*ever*—indulged?

Her round eyes swung towards June's fiancé. Judging by Randall's smile, the bewilderment she was feeling must have shown. Everett spoke, as if he could not stop himself.

'After all that tramping around that Antiques Fair, June, all those questions you asked exhibitors, all those catalogues you asked to be sent to you . . .'

'Oh, Everett,' June purred, reaching forward from the two-seater couch and patting Everett's hand, 'you're angry with me! You were such a pet, too, trailing around behind me all day.' Her voice had a 'little girl' intonation.

Girl. There it was again, Gillian realised, refusal to accept her role as a woman. What had Everett said that evening he'd arrived back so tired? 'I think it's a case of clinging to her mother, not the other way round'.

'Actually,' June was saying, 'it was my mother's idea.'

'But,' Everett could not let it rest, 'you told me that day it was your mother's suggestion that you should furnish the house with the older stuff.'

'Well, when I showed Mummy the catalogues, she said the chairs and tables and cabinets and sideboards reminded her of her grandmother's house, and she certainly didn't want to spend her days and nights among things that recalled her very stern grandparent so vividly.'

'So it's all glass and chrome and swinging basket chairs from now on?' Isobel asked, with a twinkle.

'Not quite,' June answered. 'But it's going to be the best money can buy.'

'And where do you come into all this, Randall?' Isobel queried, still smiling.

His quick shrug told more than any words. It was dismissive and uncaring.

'Shall I get some coffee, Everett?' asked Gillian, rising before he answered.

'If you want any help,' Isobel called, 'just shout.'

Gillian made for the kitchen. It was a relief to get out of the atmosphere which, to her, seemed criss-crossed with paths of tension. She was preparing the coffee and reaching for the cups and saucers from a wall cupboard when the kitchen door opened.

Randall's hands were in his jacket pockets and he urged the door closed with his shoulder. 'Don't tell me you've been working all this time on my report?'

'What else do you think I've been doing,' she snapped, fatigue corroding her temper, 'dining with another man?'

He moved towards her, removed the tray from her and tipped her chin. A finger traced beneath her eyes.

'Dark shadows, pale cheeks. I didn't tell you to work yourself into a state of exhaustion.'

'You said you wanted the work finished as soon as possible, and it's not finished yet. What else could I do but carry on?' His face was tormentingly near, his full lips hovering, his breath smelling faintly of wine.

When his lips approached hers, in their descent they caught her submitting sigh. Her mouth acted as if it had a memory of its own, parting her lips to await his kiss. The pressure increased, her jaw trembled and her arms crept to his shoulders. His hands still gripped her cheeks.

The door opened. 'Gillian,' said Everett, 'how's the coffee——' He stopped, eyes dull, lips slightly drawn in.

Randall's lips had eased from hers. Her arms were at her sides, Randall's fingers pushed under his belt. His face was expressionless as he turned to Gillian. 'I'll pay you for the overtime,' he said tersely, and walked out.

There was a look of sadness in Everett's eyes, hopelessness in his bearing.

Gillian went to him, holding him gently by the shoulders. 'I'm sorry,' she said softly. 'It meant nothing, that kiss. Randall was thanking me, nothing more.'

A deep breath, which could have been a sigh, expanded and contracted his rib cage. 'I understand, my dear. More than you think, in fact.'

'Did I—did I remind you of your ex-wife? Forgive me if I did, but——'

He took her hands from his shoulders and held them. He had managed a smile. 'If you had, I'd have followed Randall out of this room—and out of your life.' He squeezed her fingers then let them drop.

'The coffee's ready,' she told him brightly. 'Will you carry it in?'

Isobel settled into her job with ease. In the afternoons the arrival of customers into the shop seemed to Gillian to increase, and she remarked on this jokingly.

'It's my charm,' Isobel commented playfully as she sat with Gillian and Everett in the office during an afternoon tea-break.

'It certainly is,' Everett agreed, 'plus your surprisingly good knowledge of the antique trade.'

Gillian glanced at her fiancé. Since he was never sarcastic, nor insincere, he plainly meant every word. After a lightning analysis of her innermost feelings, she could discover not the faintest twinge of jealousy. A customer came in and since she had finished her tea, she went into the shop. The diversion gave her no chance to do a detection job on exactly why she did not mind her husband-to-be being so fulsome in his praise of another woman's character.

It was now less than two weeks to Everett's departure for the United States. He had made no mention of the time he had discovered Randall kissing Gillian. She wondered if he had decided that, in the circumstances, she had been in no way to blame and that Randall had initiated the kiss.

He might also, Gillian thought with some amusement, have considered that, taking into consideration their past relationship, it had been prudent of her to have submitted to her—and his—employer's amorous advances, rather than resist, since their jobs and livelihood depended on his good opinion!

Randall had returned to London, together with his fiancée and her mother. Since Everett's discovery of them in the kitchen, Randall had kept his distance. In the upstairs office he had been aloof, for which Gillian was secretly thankful. His nearness was becoming increasingly unnerving, her longing for the touch of him intensifying.

Each time Everett kissed her, she closed her eyes and tried to imagine it was Randall, but since

Randall's kisses were as different from Everett's as the Equator from the Arctic, it required an almost impossible effort of will on her part.

Four days before Everett went away, Randall returned, this time alone. He had arranged his research work in London so that he would be able to remain in residence for the whole of Everett's absence. He would keep in constant touch with his colleagues, he explained, by phone and by mail.

Everett invited him to live in his house as usual. He would be only too glad, he said, to have somebody there looking after the place.

Randall was at his desk in the upstairs office. He was explaining to Gillian the spelling of the various technical terms she would find in the course of typing his handwritten notes. He had almost finished when the telephone rang.

He reached out before Gillian could forestall him. He listened and as his brow pleated, her heartbeats grew faster. 'Just a moment,' he said to the caller, then covered the receiver. 'It's Everett. Says he's got someone called Eve on the outside line.'

Gillian's hand reached out quickly, but he held the receiver away. 'Isn't that the woman you went to stay with in Yorkshire, where the child Gary lives? Gary, who you allege is Everett's child?'

She nodded, barely able to contain her panic. Randall's questions were reasonable. If he went on asking them, how could she prevent him from discovering the truth?

'Will you let me answer that call?' she demanded shrilly, fearing his probing and wanting to speak to Eve to make sure that Gary was well. She'd missed writing her usual weekly letter, enclosing the special note with coloured-pencil sketches for Gary. He had probably worried and worried because there'd been no letter from Mummy. . . .

Randall put the receiver on the desk, gathered some

papers and left the room.

Swiftly Gillian occupied the swivel chair and seized the telephone. 'Eve?' There was a click from the telephone downstairs signifying that Everett had replaced the receiver after making sure they were connected. 'Eve, is there anything wrong?'

'All's well.' There was a short sigh. 'Just your small son pestering because his mother hasn't written. Why the delay just now in answering?'

'You went through to Everett first. Randall took the call up here.' She spoke softly in case he was around somewhere. 'He began to ask questions.' There was a worried sound from Eve. 'I—I let him think Gary was Everett's son by his ex-wife.'

'Oh, dear, o-oh, dear! Tangled web and all that. Do you think it put him off the scent?'

'I don't know, I just don't know.'

'Have a word with your ever-loving son.'

'Mummy?' The childish voice quavered, as it so often seemed to do these days. 'When can you come and live up here? I want to show you my toys, Mummy. I want you to build houses and things with me.' Gillian knew the building sets he was referring to. 'Or can I come and live where you are? Where *are* you, Mummy?'

She thought about her approaching marriage, forgetting her own feelings in the knowledge that her wedding to Everett would create a home for Gary, too. 'Not long, now, darling,' was her quiet answer. 'Then we can be a real family.'

'You, me and—who else, Mummy?'

'A—a daddy.' Try as she might, she could not visualise Everett unbending sufficiently to act the father to a young child who was not, after all, his own. 'A stepdaddy.'

There was a whoop of joy which faded as Eve took over. 'Was that wise? When's the wedding, Gillian?'

'Soon, Eve, soon.' She was so flustered she could

hardly think coherently. 'When Everett comes back from his visit to America.'

'Really? I'm glad, Gillian. You see, I've got a boy-friend. He comes to see me in the evenings, but now and then we like to go out, and I have to get a baby-sitter.'

There was no doubt about it, it was a warning, veiled though it might be, of approaching difficulties, decisions which must be made . . .

'I'm glad, Eve, very glad. I'll bear it in mind when deciding the date of the wedding. Okay with you?'

'Very much okay. Say goodbye to Mummy,' said Eve, and a tremulous young voice obeyed.

Gillian rang off and held her face in her hands. Beneath the smooth surface of her present way of living, things were changing, currents were pulling, growing stronger every day. She had to keep her head, otherwise they would sweep her away heaven knew where.

Randall returned. His mood seemed belligerent. 'If Gary is Everett's child, why did he pass that call to you? Why didn't he speak to his own son?'

'How do you know he didn't?' she asked, her voice high-pitched.

'Because I went down and asked him. The question seemed to confuse him. Why?'

She knew why, but of all people, he could not be told the reason. 'Why don't you ask *him*?' she snapped. Bracing her shoulders, she tried to push all her worries to the back of her mind. Although, she reflected wryly, she had so many not even an earth-mover would be able to achieve that!

'Can we resume where we left off?' she asked in what she hoped was a businesslike manner. 'There was one more thing to explain, wasn't there?'

Randall explained it and walked from the room.

Gillian managed to finish Randall's work by teatime

that day. During the evening she wrote the letter to Gary for which he had been waiting so impatiently, then she went to Everett's house as she had promised, to help him sort through his clothes for packing.

Using his key and mounting the stairs, she dreaded meeting Randall. Glancing at his closed door, she gave a relieved sigh, but luck was not with her as she had thought. He was talking to Everett, who, on seeing her, smiled and half rose. Randall remained in the armchair in which he was stretched out, long legs crossed at the ankles, arms lifted to support his head.

Gillian's heart spun like a globe on its axis at the sight of him. His shirt was a dark blue, making his hair seem even fairer. His jeans were creased and well-worn. His appearance flung her back into the past. This was how he had dressed in the old, golden days of their bitter-sweet loving.

His glance was cool, his eyes following the shape of her with a male detachment. When she sat, they considered her legs, making her wish she had worn jeans herself. To her annoyance, her toes curled under his assessment. It was a nervous gesture which she knew he would not miss.

When she attempted to pay him back in his own coin, letting her eyes wander over him, *he* did not curl with embarrassment. Instead, an eyebrow quirked as if asking, Are you giving me an open invitation to your bedroom? In the end, it was she who coloured, he who remained unmoved.

Everett talked of Randall's future plans. He sat cornerwise on the couch, shoulders slightly hunched, legs crossed, foot twisting, revealing tension. He was a big man, offering the security she once thought she had wanted. But now, who knew what she wanted, least of all herself?

The plans sounded so ambitious they scared her—Randall spoke of leasing large premises in the heart of London for displays of really expensive items on the market. Everett suggested starting with a section in a few famous department stores. Randall said he would consider it, but advised waiting until they saw what came of Everett's visit overseas.

'Everett,' Gillian ventured, earning an irritated frown from their employer, 'you said you wanted help with your choice of clothes.'

'Yes, my dear, yes.' He rose. 'You'll excuse us, Randall?'

Randall nodded, staying where he was, looking Gillian over again, this time with a faint touch of insolence. She felt the colour creep over her cheeks and wished she could throw something at him. Everett, at the door, saw nothing of the silent exchange, nor Randall's spiteful smile as Gillian swung away from him.

It took some time to decide which of Everett's many suits he should take with him. There were leisure clothes to sort through, suits for more formal occasions. By the time they had finished, Randall had gone to his room. Gillian made cups of tea, then, at Everett's suggestion, knocked on Randall's door.

'There's tea in the pot. Do you want a cup?' Her tone was sharp, but she could not throw off the sense of irritation his predatory examination of her had created.

'Thanks,' he answered, 'I'll have it in here.' He walked away, leaving his door open.

So he's making me wait on him in my leisure time as well as my working day! she thought angrily. As she handed him the tea, she said tartly, 'I'll charge double for that bit of overtime.'

He smiled without amusement. 'I can think of more pleasant ways of earning overtime. Unfortunately this is neither the place nor the correct circumstances. I've never yet snatched an engaged woman from under her fiancé's nose.'

'If you want a second cup,' she flung back, 'just

shout. Then I'll come back—and throw it over you!'

This time she sensed she had tipped the scales too far. Randall's lips thinned and his hand reached out to grasp her wrist.

'Gillian.' Everett stood watching. 'Your tea's getting cold.'

Randall released her, closed the door and left her facing it.

Everett walked her home, standing in the small lobby at the foot of the stairs to her apartment. With his hands on her shoulders, he thanked her for her help that evening, then kissed her lightly on the mouth.

'Don't——' he seemed to find it difficult to express himself, 'don't keep antagonising Randall, dearest,' he said at last. 'He employs us both. I'd hate to see you dismissed.'

She shook her head. 'He wouldn't do that. He'd antagonise you if he did.'

Everett shook his head. 'That wouldn't come into his calculations. He's tough, Gillian, and hard. Something's embittered him. He wouldn't hesitate to dismiss an employee, whoever it was, if that person failed to come up to his standards—or toe the line he's drawn, a very precise line, if I may say so.'

'If it means so much to you, I'll try not to let my feelings get the better of me, but——'

'My dear, you can't forever keep on having your revenge for the past. It's gone. There's only the present and the future. . . .'

He was pleading with her, and it touched her compassion. That it had not touched her love was plain by the pity that welled in her, but then she had known from the moment Randall had come back into her life that nothing and no one would ever displace or replace the love she felt for him.

It had to be faced—if Randall was soon to make a

loveless marriage, she was in no position to criticise, for so was she.

Everett left early for the airport. When Gillian offered to go with him to wave him off, he told her not to bother.

'Enjoy another hour or so in bed,' he told her, moving away from kissing her goodnight. 'You work hard enough to deserve it, and partings are not exactly happy events.'

When spontaneously she kissed him back, hugging him afterwards, he was surprised. He could not know she had just realised that, by going away, he would be removing the only reliable barrier which existed between herself and Randall.

Not that Randall would touch her, she told herself later as she prepared for bed. Since that telephone call from Eve, he had been as distant as a stranger. His very remoteness worked on her nervous system like a fretsaw. She wanted to fling herself at him, run her nails down his cheeks, kiss him as ardently as she used to kiss him when they were lovers.

Two days after Everett had gone the telephone rang in the office at the rear of the shop. It was mid-morning and Gillian was serving a customer. Randall came out of the office, taking the delicate porcelain jug from her hands.

'It's for you,' he said. 'I'll take over.' He did not look pleased, but, she argued, he never did these days.

'Who is it?' she asked over her shoulder, but he did not answer.

'Oh, Eve!' Gillian said into the telephone. 'Is there something——?'

'Wrong? No, everything's right! Jimmy's proposed. I know it seems quick work, but he's a divorcee and I'm lonely, so we thought, Why wait?'

Gillian closed her eyes, curling her hand into a fist on the desk. 'That's wonderful, Eve. How soon? A couple of weeks? So—so you'll want me to do something about Gary?'

'Well, we talked about it, and decided we'd postpone our honeymoon until after yours, then we'd have ours when you come and collect—you-know-who. He doesn't know who I'm talking to, by the way. Hope I haven't disturbed you, but I just had to tell someone the good news!'

'I'm glad for you, Eve, really glad.'

'You'll like him on sight, Gillian, just like I did. Mustn't keep you. Keep us informed of events.'

'I will. Kiss Gary for me, Eve.'

When Gillian put the phone down, her hand was trembling. She pressed it to her cheek. Events were moving too fast. Things were so unsettled, she wasn't certain of anything any more.

'And you said the child was Everett's.' She swung on the chair to face the door. Randall was propped against it. The shop was empty. 'Yet you said, Kiss him for me.'

'Well,' she bluffed, 'what's so wrong with that? Isn't it lucky that I—I love him, since—since he's going to be mine soon? Since I'm going to be his mother?'

For an unendurable moment Randall stared at her. Had he guessed? He stayed silent on the subject, motioning with his head. 'Get out of that chair. I want to use the desk. Get back in the shop.'

She fought with the desire to scream at him, Stop ordering me about! I'm a human being, not a misbehaving domestic animal. Instead, she obeyed, walking past him, head high, drawing herself in so as not to touch him.

That afternoon he piled work upon her. 'This is urgent. I want it by this evening.'

'All that?' she asked, aghast. 'But it'll take me hours!'

'At the speed you type, I doubt it. Make a start now and carry on until you finish.'

The chair swivelled as she watched him go.

'Suppose I don't manage it?'

'You will,' he replied tersely, without turning his head.

By teatime, she was already feeling the strain. As she cleared away her meal, Randall arrived.

'No,' she snapped, forestalling him, 'I haven't finished the work. I'm only halfway through. If—if I don't get it finished, I'll carry on in the morning.'

'You work in the shop in the mornings. Finish it tonight.'

Don't keep antagonising Randall. Everett's words echoed somewhere in her head. But what were echoes when reality was a desperately troubled mind, aching fingers, a weary body and a frustrated love for the man who gazed coldly at her from across the room?

'I'm tired,' she hit out, 'tired to my very bones. My hands won't do what my brain tells them. I'll carry on until I have to stop, then I'll stop. And there's nothing you can do about it!'

'There's plenty, Gillian. You'll finish that work tonight or you'll find yourself homeless and jobless in the morning.'

Her breath wouldn't come, her hand held her throat. 'What's got into you, Rand?' she whispered. 'You're *inhuman*! You can't mean what you're saying.'

'I mean every word. So,' his smile twisted, 'you'd better get back to the typewriter, hadn't you? Call me when it's finished.'

For some minutes after he had gone she couldn't move. Then she came to life, loosened her shoulder muscles and stretched her arms and did as he had told her.

At two o'clock in the morning she called him on the phone, hoping spitefully that he was asleep, but the call was answered immediately. 'Well?' He knew who it was at once.

'I've finished.'

The phone crashed down at his end and she was left

listening to the emptiness. Dragging herself to bed, she lay for some time, too exhausted to sleep. Eventually she sank into oblivion, dreading what the next day might bring.

It brought no thanks, no gratitude, and another long, handwritten report. When he gave it to her she thought, Not again! She kept silent, however, determined never again to reveal any weakness in front of him. This time she typed through her mealtime, replenishing her energy with coffee. At midnight she rang him.

'I've finished,' she told him. 'I missed my meal, I'm dropping with fatigue——' He rang off. He had not even thanked her!

Slipping her nightgown over her head, Gillian sat on the dressing-table stool and drank the mug of hot milk she had made herself. She had been beyond food by the time her work had ended. Putting down the mug, she turned to the mirror and ran a comb through her long fair hair. During the day she had worn it up, fastened with the aid of combs.

Tiredness had not darkened the light blue of her eyes, nor spoiled the shape of her mouth. But there was an anxiety in her expression which made her cheeks seem thinner and tightened the set of her lips.

The door opened and she turned quickly, frightened. The intruder was only too familiar to her. All the same, anger lit her eyes as she challenged,

'What do you want? I've finished your work. Or have you got some more I must do before I have my night's sleep?' She nodded at the pile of paper he held.

'Don't be a fool, Gillian.' He looked tired, too, she noticed, but she forced her sympathy back into a pocket in her mind. Why should she be sorry for him if he wasn't sorry for her?

'Yes, that's what I am—a fool. I push myself to my limits and all I get is more work pushed at me. No thanks, no gratitude——'

'You're being well paid,' Randall answered curtly. 'What else do you want? Unless——' His eyes made their wandering way over the curves half revealed beneath the filmy gown. 'Unless you've *dressed* for my benefit?'

Flustered now, feeling her pulses beating hard, she looked down at herself. 'I always go to bed like this.'

When she saw his eyes narrow, she knew she had asked for trouble with such a statement. He put aside the papers and came towards her. 'Do you?' he responded. 'I know differently. When we used to go to bed in my room in that house I shared, you didn't even bother to bring a nightdress with you.'

'Why are you making it sound so sordid? We made love because we loved, because we knew how little time we had—you had . . . Or so we thought.' Her voice tailed off and she wrapped her arms about her. Her body felt haunted; she sensed the ghost-touch of him; remembered the first time they had ever come together, the pain, the ecstasy . . .

He moved quickly, seizing her arms, jerking her to her feet. 'And you shortened that time by running away. I didn't even have the chance to whisper, There's hope, my darling, we may have a future, after all.' His grip tightened as he shook her. 'You were a coward. You escaped before you were contaminated. Confess it's true.'

'But it's not true!' Her voice was a cry as she struggled to free herself from his hard, bruising grasp.

'Then tell me why!'

Her body went limp, but still his grip persisted, pulling her against him, making her feel his masculinity. 'I can't, I can't.' Her lips were dry, her head throbbing. 'Rand,' large eyes found his, rebounding off the glitter in his gaze, 'I'm tired to my depths. Let me rest, *please*!'

He let her go and she staggered to the bed, lying across it, uncaring that beneath the nightgown, every part of her body could be seen by him. He moved and she tensed. But he was retrieving the papers, smiling humourlessly at her nervousness.

'Tomorrow I'm returning to London. I'll be away a few days. Help in the shop all day.' He went out, without a single glance back.

CHAPTER SEVEN

'YOU look,' said Isobel next afternoon, 'to use an old phrase, as if you've been pulled through a hedge backwards!'

'Thanks a lot,' Gillian replied, smiling faintly, cleaning the silver.

'If you look like that when Everett comes back, he'll send you on a prolonged holiday to recuperate before he marries you!'

'Your flattery is making me blush,' Gillian returned. 'But I know I look tired.' She returned to polishing the silver salver. 'Randall's been standing over me like a slavemaster with a verbal whip!' She had spoken lightly, but in her heart she knew it was true.

'Well, take it easy while he's away,' Isobel advised. 'I can manage without you, you know.'

Gillian shrugged. 'Randall told me to work afternoons, but——'

Isobel took charge, pointing upstairs. 'Collect a jacket or something. Here are my car keys.' She took them from her handbag. 'Get yourself out into the country for an hour or so. Park the car, go walkabout.'

Gillian laughed. 'You win! I hope Randall doesn't decide to come back while I'm out.'

'I do believe you're afraid of the man!'

'Not really. I——' She took the car keys. 'Thanks a lot, Isobel.'

As she drove through the hills and farmland of Dorset, she thought, If I am frightened of Randall, it's because of what he does to me. I'm scared of giving myself away, letting him know how I love him. She parked the car and walked, finding the summit of a hill and gazing at the far-reaching patchwork of green fields, the blue sky and scattered cloud formations.

While her eyes recorded every detail of the view, with a farmhouse here, a field of cattle there, ancient churches with their Saxon towers and pointed spires sprinkled, minute as models, across the whole panorama, her mind was busy thinking about Eve's coming marriage and how, very soon, she would have to bring Gary back with her to share her own life.

Her marriage to Everett could not be too long delayed. It had to be faced that soon she would be his wife. There had been so little lovemaking between them that she simply did not know how his touch would affect her, how she would respond to his passionate kisses. Her scanning eyes and her wandering thoughts stopped abruptly. Would there be any passionate kisses?

'Ask Everett why his ex-wife divorced him,' Randall had said some time ago. It was something she had never ventured to question Everett about. Had it, perhaps, not been the woman's fault after all? Was it not the lack of a ring on her finger that stopped Everett from making love to her? Was it, instead, the fact that he possessed little or even no sex drive?

Fiercely she shook her head, as if to shake out such thoughts. It was too late now to consider such matters. For Gary's sake a wedding had to take place. Everett offered the stability and firm base which a child needed on which to grow and develop. If the question, And what about marital love? did put its foot in the door of her mind, she firmly and resolutely pushed against it until the door slammed shut.

Randall returned after a few days' absence. With him came a resumption of the relentless pressure of work. His brain seemed to have been refreshed by the break and words flowed from his pen on to paper. He produced sheet after sheet of closely handwritten notes. Every word was clear and precise—only too clear, Gillian thought, as day after day, sometimes until midnight, she read them with tired eyes.

'I see Everett's enjoying his stay in the States,' Isobel greeted her one lunchtime as she came to take over the shop. 'Living it up in a big hotel, meeting the rich and so on.'

Gillian looked at her blankly. 'How do you know? Did you answer a call from him for Randall or something?'

Isobel covered her mouth. 'Sorry, I thought you'd had a card from him, too. I felt sure——' She rubbed the back of her hair with a slightly agitated movement. 'I expect he posted the two cards together and mine got here first.'

'Yes, yes, that's it,' Gillian agreed quickly, with a smile. 'It can easily happen.' All the same, she had been wondering when Everett would write to her, since he had promised to do so within a day or two of arriving there.

Writing. . . . As she climbed the stairs to make some lunch for herself, she remembered that it was her day for writing her letter to Gary. After eating a snack, she carefully turned the handle of the office door. There had been no sound from the room, but that did not mean that Randall was not in occupation. Sometimes he sat, feet on desk, staring at nothing, just thinking.

She had grown almost to dread the sound of his feet on the stairs, his shout for her to come in and go through the latest batch of notes with him. The room was empty and she raked in a drawer, taking out a writing pad and a handful of coloured pencils.

'Darling Gary,' she typed, 'how are you? Do you play with sand at your nursery school? Do you wear an apron when you paint pictures?' She knew that Eve would read her letter to him. 'One day, before very long, I hope you will be able to come and live with me here in this nice little town. The sea is not so very far away and we can swim in it.'

Gillian stopped, picking up one coloured pencil after another and drawing pictures which she hoped he would understand. There were waves and cliffs and buckets and spades. 'Auntie Eve,' she typed, 'is getting married very soon now. But she will look after you until I can come and collect you. All my love, Mummy.'

Removing the paper from the machine, she heard footsteps mounting the stairs. With a beating heart she folded the letter and thrust it into the drawer, banging it shut.

'Working already?' The sarcastic tone told of his mood. How long had he been standing in the doorway? Had he seen her hurried actions and if so, had his curiosity been aroused?

'Just a letter,' she told him, 'a personal one. But,' she turned on a bright smile, 'I'm ready for work now.'

'You said it. I hope you won't regret the statement.' He produced a bulging folder from behind his back. 'This draft report came in the post this morning. I've corrected it, added bits and taken some away. I want it finished today.' He put the folder beside her. 'Now, has that taken the smile off your face?'

Turning the pages, she frowned unbelievingly. 'You can't mean it! You must know you're asking the impossible.'

'To quote a well-known saying, "The difficult takes a little time: the impossible takes a little longer".' His tone was implacable, his eyes hard.

'In other words, "Get on with it." '

'Exactly.' He went out and she heard him leave the apartment.

With unsteady fingers Gillian turned the pages. The corrections appeared to have been made under pressure. They were certainly not as clear as they usually were. Which meant, she assessed, that the work would take her much longer to type.

Her head went back and she closed her eyes. There were two options open to her. Either she carried on and did the work with her usual speed and attention to detail—or she quit her job, here and now. For a few moments the second option beckoned. Then she thought of Gary and her approaching responsibilities.

Everett had not yet raised the matter of a second date for their postponed marriage. Now that Eve was about to be married herself, it was necessary to relieve her as quickly as possible of Gary's presence. In any case, she thought, gazing ruefully at the work that awaited her, she acknowledged in her heart that the first option was, in reality, the only one. When you loved a man as deeply as she loved Randall, you did everything possible to please him.

Gillian typed until it was time for her evening meal. This she had hurriedly in the kitchen, putting aside the dishes and rushing back to work. It was two hours later that she began to make mistakes. The typewriter was some years old, which meant that correcting her errors took time. That time mounted up and so did the minutes, into two more hours.

When the phone rang, she answered it irritably.

'How are things going?' a lazy voice enquired.

'They're not going,' she choked. 'They've almost come to a stop!' Then she rammed the phone down.

After typing three pages seemingly without error, she decided to read them over, unable to believe her luck. It had, she discovered, been right to do so. Each page held four or five unnoticed mistakes and she almost cried when the corrections looked so bad she had to type each page again. Determinedly she typed on, even when footsteps sounded and the office door opened.

'Go away,' she muttered through her teeth, 'go away or I'll——'

'I'm staying,' was the quiet reply, and Randall sat himself at the other desk, pushing folders and files aside. As he worked within touching distance, Gillian found herself growing so tense her fingers became stiff. Her lips were sore from maltreatment by her teeth. 'I'll have to get out of here,' she told herself, and did so, feeling Randall's surprised gaze on her back.

Soaking her hands in warm water, she closed her eyes and took deep breaths. Does he know what he's reducing me to? she thought. The armchair helped to loosen her muscles as she rested her head and shoulders and flexed her fingers.

Having taken a long, cold drink of milk, she returned, only partially refreshed. As she walked in, Randall asked, 'How much longer?'

'Days,' she hit back, 'years. I'll grow old and grey finishing it. And so will you,' she added nastily, hoping he would take the hint and leave, but he did not move.

Soon her eyes grew blurred. The typed letters seemed to tip drunkenly, and her fingers were tapping out indecipherable messages. It was when she realised her fingers had slipped to the wrong line of keys that her control broke.

'No,' she shrieked, '*no*! I refuse to type another word!' Her fist pounded on the desk, and Randall swung round. 'I've worked myself almost into a zombie over your precious work,' she stormed. 'You've driven me like a slavedriver, using your power as an employer like a whip!' Her fingers curled and she raised them, palms upward, in front of him. 'Haven't you any humanity left? What's happened to you? Haven't you got a heart any more? What have I done to make you hate me so?'

Slowly his pen was lowered to the desk. He got up and stood in front of her, his fists on his hips. 'What have you done?' He jerked the desk drawer open and took out her letter to Gary. 'Isn't this indictment enough?'

'You searched through my things while I was out of the room!'

'It was plain you had something to hide. I watched you from the door.'

'You're a sneak, Randall. And I don't know what you mean by "indictment". I haven't committed a crime, just written a letter to a—to a child.'

'A child of whom you seem to be extremely fond. *All my love—Mummy*,' he quoted. 'And you expect me to believe that the boy is Everett's by his former wife?' He threw the letter aside and gripped her arms. His mouth grew taut, his jaw angular. It was the blazing anger in his eyes that made her afraid.

'Yes, I do expect you to believe that,' she flung back bravely. 'Why is it so impossible for a future stepmother to love her future stepson? I told you once, I love children. I want them. . . .'

A devilish light flooded his eyes. 'Then we'll see if we can provide them for you, shall we?'

She went white and still. 'What do you mean?'

He ignored her question and tightened his grip instead. She winced at the pain. 'You're not only a cheat, you're a coward and a liar! The child's yours and Everett's, as I suspected.'

Gillian's head was shaking, loosening her hair from its fastening. He held her from him, looking her over. 'I'll give you one more chance to tell me the truth. Is the boy Everett's and his ex-wife's, or Everett's and yours?'

Her hands covered her face, knowing it was a time of reckoning. If she swore Gary was Everett's, she knew Randall would ask him for confirmation. Everett knew she had already lied to Randall about Gary being his. But it would be completely unfair to Everett to put him in the position of having to tell—and act—a lie.

Yet if she continued to deny that Gary was hers and Everett's, there could be only one conclusion Randall could possibly come to. The age would be right, the facial similarity, her love for the child . . . they would all combine to lead him to the obvious answer—that the boy was hers—*and his*!

Removing her hands, she looked into Randall's face, and what she saw there made her tremble. If she so much as gave away even a hint of the truth, Gary would be lost to her for ever.

Her clasped hands were moist as they lifted to her mouth. 'M-mine and Everett's,' she whispered, and watched as his blue eyes went dark with rage.

'You bitch,' he bit out, 'you unscrupulous, immoral little tramp! So you broke up a marriage by having an affair with the husband, and then brazenly had his child. Then you tried—still are trying—to hide your transgression behind the smokescreen of the resulting divorce!'

His hands moved to her cheeks, where his fingers and nails pressed unbearably, contorting her features. 'You've had it easy so far, haven't you? You've got a devoted fiancé, who's the father of your child, who's willing to marry you and give that child a home, *and* support you, despite the fact that you broke up his marriage.'

He strained her head even farther back. 'Well, fate's caught up with you, my one-time lover. And you're going to take your punishment like the hard-bitten little traitor you are.'

'It's not like that, Rand. I wish I could explain, but——'

'It would be all lies. You cheated me, then you cheated Everett out of his marriage . . .'

He was pushing her backwards, propelling her out of the office. She tried turning her head to see where they were going, but the strain of his hold on her face brought tears springing and falling. Her hands lifted to cling to his sweater, then he was easing her through a door.

The bed gave as he pushed her onto it. He forced open the blouse she was wearing and pulled it off. She was paralysed with apprehension mixed with desire, but she managed to swing her legs off the bed. A moment later she regretted the action. Randall's hands were at her jeans fastening, then they were thrown to the floor.

He lifted her legs back on to the bed, then jerked his sweater over his head. The sight of his strong body was a shock of pleasure. There was flesh on his bones, strength in his muscles, and there was no doubt at all that he was a vigorous, healthy male. Where once his skin had been white and almost bloodless, now it was tanned and tough.

When his fingers went to his belt fastening, she knew fully his intention. She could not let it happen!

'No,' she cried, 'I won't let you, Rand! It's Everett I'm engaged to, not you. I'm not going to be unfaithful to him before we're married.' She sat up, stretching out her arms. 'Leave me alone, *please*! Can't you see, I owe *him* my loyalty, not you any more. You've got your own fiancée——'

'Loyalty?' he sneered. 'What do you know about loyalty? Or faithfulness? They're not in your make-up.'

He stood before her, and his masculinity could not be ignored. She tried to avert her eyes from his magnetism, but they were drawn inexorably back.

'Everett's giving me a home,' she declared, 'and security and a solid family background for Gary——'

'Gary!' She had said the wrong thing. Randall strode round to the bedside table, seized the photograph and studied it. Gillian caught her breath. Would he see, would he recognise his own features?

It seemed his eyes were looking through the flames of his anger. He hurled the photograph across the room and there was a crash of broken glass. He had destroyed the picture of his own son! She went to scramble off the bed.

'You've broken it! That was a diabolical thing to do!'

He was on the bed beside her, urging her back, stilling her flailing arms and legs by the pressure of his own. 'You've had this coming,' he snapped. 'You want me as much as I want you and I'm going to have you, my girl, body and soul.'

His mouth descended, capturing hers even as she turned her head from side to side. His fingers found the bra fastening, urging it off. A moment later she was as naked as he was. The feel of him against her filled her with joy, yet strengthened her fight to free herself, because she knew it was wrong. Randall didn't love her now—if he ever had. 'I'm cured of you,' he'd said.

Her struggles were futile in the face of his greater power and she felt her resistance crumble as the deep fatigue she had been fighting caught up with her. His teeth against her lips made them part. As she gasped at the force of his kiss, his hands made a merciless tour of her body and she cried out at his savagery.

'Rand,' she moaned, 'oh, Rand!' His mouth lifted fractionally, allowing her to speak. 'If you knew, you'd understand, you'd understand . . .' His teeth caught at her shoulder and she writhed beneath him. 'Don't spoil the memories,' she pleaded, 'the beautiful memories. They're all we have left.'

He lifted his head and stared contemptuously into her face. '*Beautiful* memories,' he derided, 'when you've defiled them by your actions since they happened between us? Lying to me about your true relationship with Everett, pretending the child was his and his ex-wife's, not yours and his.'

Randall's hold on her had tightened and she began to sob at the pain. She felt the hard thud of his heart as his chest pressed against her breasts. There was the surge of his muscles as he changed position, and he caught her quivering lips with his. He was slowly, surely, draining the life out of her, but even so her mind sang at the renewed contact with his body which she loved more now, if that was possible, than in the past.

Their legs entangled and it was thigh against thigh. His head moved and he kissed the rounded breasts which had nurtured his child, and she knew an ecstasy beyond belief as she felt his lips teasing them into hardening response.

Was he remembering the past, too? He was, in spite of himself, abandoning the role of barbaric pursuer and seeker of vengeance and turning lover, stroking her, kissing her to vibrant life. When he took her, the ecstatic, thrilling responses of her body to his forceful possession lifted her to a golden world. Reality receded, nothing mattered except that they had returned at last to each other's arms, giving, receiving and giving again and again.

As the joy of reunion, having reached a pinnacle, slowly retreated, Randall lay with his head on her breasts, his breath skimming her tingling skin. A face formed in her mind, young, fair and bright-eyed. *Is that my daddy?* the eager voice asked.

She knew, with infinite sadness, that the day would never come when she could answer, 'Yes, he's here at last.'

As daylight touched the room with colour, she was conscious of his leaving her. Her arm had stretched out, trying to stop him, but she had barely been awake. A hand took hers, the touch of lips warmed it fleetingly, then the covers were pulled over her.

When, an hour or two later, she awoke fully, she found herself alone. Although it was time to wash and dress, she lay for a few moments savouring the tranquillity of her body and the quiet contentment within her mind. Only as she looked at the radiance of her reflection did her conscience stir, reminding her of her fiancé.

If becoming one with the man you loved was being unfaithful, then unfaithful she had been. In her thoughts she vowed to Everett, It will never, in my whole life, happen again.

Hurrying downstairs to open the shop, she found Isobel in the office. 'I've just arrived,' Isobel explained. 'I had an urgent call from Randall. He had to go to London, he said, and would I be able to come in every day for the next week.'

Gillian hid her disappointment with an effort. 'Why? I thought I served in the shop mornings and you in the——'

'He asked me to give you a message. Take the rest of the week off, he said. Keep out of the shop and take it easy. He told me that last night he'd worked you into a state of near-collapse and that you nearly passed out on him.'

Gillian frowned. So that was Randall's description of what had taken place between them! It was certainly what he would tell Everett, and she would never contradict it.

Isobel seemed to expect an answer. 'Well, it's true, I suppose. I've worked like mad lately, typing his notes, until midnight sometimes.' She smiled and hoped it was not too bright, giving away her inner happiness. 'I could certainly use a few days' rest. What about the office?'

'Leave it all to me. Anything I can't deal with, I'll ask you about.' Isobel glanced outside. 'Looks like our first customer of the day. Now, do what teacher tells you and go out to play.'

'Any post?' Gillian asked hurriedly as the door opened. Isobel shook her head. 'No card from Everett?' Isobel made a face as if she couldn't understand it.

Still puzzled, Gillian went into the office until Isobel was free again. When she eventually came in, Gillian asked her casually, 'Any idea why Randall returned to London? I mean, he said nothing to me, and I hadn't finished the work last night when I——'

'Flaked out on him,' Isobel finished. 'Could be because his fiancée phoned him this morning. I was standing near him and heard her say, "I've missed you so much, da-arling." ' Isobel mimicked June's way of talking. 'Then he said, "I'll be with you as soon as I can make it." He made sure I was free mornings, gave me that message for you and just went.'

Went at his fiancée's call, Gillian thought miserably. The idea was painful, but how could she, even for a moment, have imagined that one night spent making love to her would have brought Randall's feelings for her back to life? Just one of many, he had described her not so long ago. With his wedding day approaching, it must be more true than ever.

'Everett's card,' Isobel put her hand on Gillian's arm, 'it'll come tomorrow, I'm sure it will. You know how mail can get delayed, especially from overseas.'

'I'm not really worried. I'd just like to know he's okay——'

'And missing you as much as you're missing him.'

Gillian nodded, finding it an easier way of salving her conscience than actually saying 'yes'. Her mind drifted back to the events of the night, recalling Randall's anger, the way he had hurled Gary's picture across the room . . . That was it!

'I'll get away for a couple of days,' she told Isobel. 'I'll take the break Randall said I should have. I'll go north and see—friends.'

'Fine,' Isobel responded, smiling. 'I can cope, honestly.'

Gillian smiled her thanks, then made for her apartment and reached for the telephone.

CHAPTER EIGHT

'AUNTIE EVE'S getting married tomorrow!' Gary danced in front of his mother, then wrapped his arms about her hips, hugging her.

'Isn't it wonderful, darling?' Gillian answered, stroking his hair. To Eve she said, 'Have you booked for tomorrow night in a good hotel somewhere, as I suggested on the phone?'

Eve nodded. 'I'm glad you were able to come. Your few days off fitted in well, didn't they? Like my hair? I had it specially styled to suit my hat. Hope it suits my face, too! Jimmy hasn't seen it yet, not till after the ceremony. I hope it won't make him sorry he married me.'

Eve was prattling in her happiness and Gillian smiled, listening and wishing . . . wishing she were in Eve's shoes. Was this how she would feel on the eve of her marriage to Everett? She refused to answer her own question, looking down at the small boy who gripped her hand and who gazed up at her as if he could not fill his eyes with enough of her. Did he really miss her as much as that, or was he caught up in the undercurrents which ebbed and flowed beneath the muted excitement of Eve's behaviour?

Gillian put Gary to bed. He was reluctant to let her leave, but she was firm with him, knowing that staying with him until he slept was something which, in the circumstances, it would be very unwise to start.

Downstairs, Eve flitted about, apparently unable to sit still. 'Have you packed an overnight case?' Gillian asked her as she dusted, moved ornaments, then dusted again.

'Thrown a few things into a bag,' Eve answered. 'Gillian, I wish you'd come to the wedding.'

'Thanks for asking, but I'll look after Gary.'

'I could ring my lady help and say I'd like her to take care of him, after all.'

'Look, I'm here to free you from the burden of having a small, highly excitable boy on your hands. But I give you permission to bring me back a piece of wedding cake. I'm very partial to those!'

Eve smiled. 'You'll be having one of your own, soon.'

The words did not warm Gillian's heart as Eve probably thought they had.

In the night, Gary cried out. Gillian was pulling on a wrap and was into his bedroom before the cry was repeated. 'Mummy, Mummy,' Gary muttered hoarsely. 'I thought you'd gone away, like you said my daddy went away.' Gillian's arms were round him, and he was curled in her lap. His young, fair head rested against her breast and she was reminded of another fair head resting there, seeking tranquillity . . . was it only last night?

Eve came in, trailing her dressing-gown. 'Everything under control?'

Gillian nodded and whispered, 'Does he do this often, Eve?'

For a moment it seemed as though Eve was not going to reply. At last she answered, 'At fairly frequent intervals.'

'Oh, Eve, I'm so sorry! Why didn't you tell me?'

'What could you have done? He's in my care, isn't he, so I have to cope.'

'Eve, I promise, it won't be long now. When Everett gets back, I'll ask him to fix a date. I do hope he,' indicating the clinging form on her lap, 'doesn't annoy Jimmy.' Eve was shaking her head, but Gillian persisted, 'After all, newlyweds——'

'Don't fret, love. We're not shining-eyed youngsters. We've both been married before. Anyway, somebody,' she nodded at Gary, 'might feel reassured to have a man in the house. Father figure and all that.'

Gillian nodded, put a finger to her lips and lifted her son on to his bed, tucking him in. He slept on, looking angelic. She placed a light kiss on his forehead and followed Eve out.

Next morning Eve assured Gillian that she had gone straight back to sleep. 'I don't look the worse for wear, do I?'

'You look the proverbial radiant bride. Jimmy will be proud of you.'

'The car's here!' Eve exclaimed, gazing out of the front window. 'Wish me luck, love.'

'You know I do.' Gillian kissed her cheek, then lifted Gary, whereupon Eve kissed him.

Eve started to run to the car, slowed down, then walked gracefully through the open gate to the road. The family friend who had agreed to be best man got out, saw her into the car, giving a sweeping bow, then waved to Gillian.

The car, white ribbons fluttering, drove away.

That day Gillian felt closer to her little son than she had ever done before. She played his games, helped him in his rudimentary efforts to build houses with plastic kits, pushed his toy cars and fire engines and 'giant' trucks from one end of the kitchen to the other.

Later, after the midday meal, she took him into the nearest town. It was raining and they ran, hoods up, hand in hand, along the street to the main department store. When Gary complained he couldn't see 'the things up there' on the display counters, Gillian carried him.

In the toy department he wandered, his hand still clinging to hers, as if in a dream world. They made their way to the restaurant where, as a special treat, they ate cream cakes and ice cream and drank milk shakes.

As she bathed him and dressed him in his nightclothes, it was her mind that had drifted into a dream state. It was a world, she thought, listening to Gary's chatter and answering him, where he was always there, and so was she, and his father would be coming in soon from a day's work. They would kiss and eat and watch television. They would go to bed and make love, the kind of love they had made last night, only better, sweeter and passionately intense. . . .

That night, Gary slept through until morning. Now and then Gillian crept in to watch his face, vulnerable, intelligent, with a heartbreaking promise of his father's good looks and character to come.

The phone rang early next morning. 'How are you getting along?' Eve enquired.

'Fine. How was the wedding?'

'Very fine,' was the laughing reply. 'Is it all right with you, Gillian, if Jimmy and I go along to his flat today? He's been packing, but there's loads to be done. Oh, and about tonight——'

'Stay there,' Gillian stated firmly. 'Sleep on the floor if the bed's too crowded.'

There was laughter and gratitude for her understanding. 'Anyone would think,' Eve commented, 'that you'd been married yourself! Hey, sorry about that, love. You know what I mean, don't you?'

'Of course. Enjoy yourselves. See you tomorrow, maybe?'

'Tomorrow for certain,' Eve agreed, and rang off.

'We'll go for a picnic today,' Gillian announced to an absorbed Gary, who sat on the floor playing with his toys, as close to her as he could get. They made for the wide open expanses of the moors, using Eve's car as she had suggested.

As she gazed at the sweeping, untamed panorama of dale and moorland, Gillian knew she was dreading the moment of parting. The windswept, lonely scene all around equated with an equally wild, lonely area of her mind. The wilderness inside her was even more daunting than that around her.

The future had become frighteningly uncertain. The path of her life had grown faint, even disappearing. She was more lost than those sheep grazing, contented and untroubled, on the fellside across the valley. Even when the sun started to descend and the resulting chill told her it was time to return, she had not rediscovered that path.

Gary cried when she left next morning. He clung and sobbed, the fingers of his two hands meeting round her arm in a desperate bid to prevent her from going. On the train, the scene replayed itself vividly in her mind like a video recording.

Although Eve had held the small, sobbing body and her new husband had crouched down and talked gently to the boy, Gillian sensed within Jimmy a man's impatience of a child's seemingly illogical behaviour. How long would he tolerate in his married life a stranger's child?

A nagging sense of urgency quickened her breathing. If Randall ever discovered the truth about Gary, what would he do? She resolved that, as soon as Everett came home, she must ask him to discuss another date for their wedding. The decision alone was sufficient to ease her deep anxiety. She did not even consider that in her haste to prevent Gary from being snatched into his father's custody, she might be condemning herself to a lifetime of marital mediocrity.

Isobel greeted Gillian joyfully. 'There's a letter from Everett,' she exclaimed. 'It looks thick and interesting. There, aren't you pleased?'

Gillian accepted it with thanks and a wide smile of pretended delight. Taking her suitcases to her bedroom, she sank on to the bed and opened Everett's letter. She did not remove it from the envelope immediately, but closed her eyes, reliving again the scene just before her departure. How long would Gary's cries ring in her ears? For all the days and nights until she was with him again?

Sighing, Gillian started reading the letter. The first few sentences caught her interest as she read about his experiences and the warm welcome he had been given, even by complete strangers. It was about a quarter of the way through the letter that her attention was truly caught.

'Now I've come to what I really want to say,' Everett's letter ran, 'and I hardly know how to put it. I can only write with frankness and honesty and I can only hope, also, that it doesn't hurt you too much.'

Gillian ignored the rumblings inside her which warned her that she had eaten too little for her midday meal at the main line station in London, before catching the train to the south-west.

'When it all started, I'm not sure, but it was not long after Randall West came into our lives. All the time, and I'm sure without your knowing it, I've been conscious of this feeling between you and Randall. Thinking about it time after time, Gillian, I'm sure that, from your point of view if not his, it's not all over between you. I've become convinced that you love him, and that I come a long way down the scale where your emotions are concerned.

'To be honest again,' Everett went on, 'I just can't take it any more. I can't stand the feeling of tension, the looks that pass between you, the strength of the currents pulling you this way and that. I have to say, although I know I'm letting you down because of Gary, that I don't think our engagement can continue.'

Gillian lowered the letter to her lap and closed her eyes. Now she realised the reason for that sense of foreboding which had dogged her these last few days—somehow, deep in her subconscious self, she must have known this was coming. There were a few more paragraphs of apology and promising to talk to her when he returned before telling anyone of the break between them.

For the rest of the day she put on a plausible act of contented fiancée having received a long letter of affection and declarations of everlasting love from the man to whom she was soon to be married. It was when she was alone in her bedroom that night that she recalled the last time she had slept in the bed.

In his letter, Everett had said, *I'm sure that from your point of view if not his, it's not all over between you. I'm convinced you love him. . . .* With her hands covering her compressed lips, she thought sadly that Everett possessed more perception than she had credited him with. When she had submitted so joyfully to Randall's lovemaking a few nights ago, she knew now that she had had no need to feel any guilt about being 'unfaithful' to Everett. He had, it seemed, been drifting away from her for some time.

The days passed, the number of customers started to increase and business was booming. Gillian had spoken a few times to Gary on the phone. This, Eve said, seemed to cheer him. 'When am I going to live with you and a daddy?' he kept asking, and she could only reply, hating herself for making a false promise, 'Soon, Gary, soon.'

One evening in the middle of the following week, Gillian was curled in her night clothes and dressing-gown on the living-room couch. She had been mending some of Gary's socks and T-shirts which she had brought back with her.

Although her weekly salary was good for the work for which she was employed, it did not allow for a renewal of Gary's clothes as soon as they showed signs of needing repair. It was expensive enough keeping up with his rapid growth, she thought, without replacement simply because of wear and tear.

Putting aside her mending at last, she let her thoughts roam. The problems were mounting and, probably because of the time of night, her brain reared at the very thought of attempting to solve them. Her mind must have found the easy way out, since the next thing she knew was a voice saying,

'The industrious and devoted mother takes a well-earned rest.'

'Everett?' It was the first word that came into her mind, the only explanation she could, in the daze of waking, think of for a man in her bedroom. Then her eyes came fully open and she realised she was not in her bedroom and that the man gazing down at her was not Everett but Randall. Of course, she thought, who but Randall could give such a sarcastic greeting after an absence of over a week?

Her face was flushed and not only with a too-swift emergence from sleep. Pleasure at the sight of the man she loved had put the heat in her face as well as her body. Her heart responded to his sudden presence as a flower to the morning sun and her instinct was to open her arms wide and cling to him as tightly as Gary had clung to her. *Don't leave me again!* she wanted to cry to him as Gary had done.

Her legs swung to the floor and she faced him boldly, although she knew that by doing so she was living dangerously. One lift of his finger and no question about it, she would be his for the taking. In order to contradict any impression she might be giving, however, that she was his, body and soul, she said, just a little tartly,

'So you managed to tear yourself from your loved one's arms and come back to see how your antiques business was getting on.'

'Sour, my love? Have you missed me, then, in spite of the fact that you called me Everett, although he's thousands of miles away.' His mouth curled faintly and a finger flicked a curl which had strayed over her cheek.

In a flash of remembrance, June's words came to

her. '"I've missed you so much, da-arling,"' she drawled, and smiled provokingly back.

At first Randall frowned, then he smiled, his eyes narrowing. 'June's remark to me as passed on by the grapevine—name of Isobel. Well,' a glint of revenge showed in his partly-veiled blue eyes, 'how many phone calls have you had from New York from your loved one?'

He had managed to put her on the defensive. 'Maybe he doesn't like spending your money like water, on a purely personal matter. Anyway, I've had a long, long letter from him——'

'One, not one a day?'

He had floored her again and taken away her smile. If he discovered what that one letter had contained. . . .

'I hear you had a short holiday last week. Don't look so surprised. *I* use the telephone, even if Everett doesn't. I kept in touch with Isobel about the shop. When she told me she was managing perfectly well on her own, I asked why alone, and she told me.' His hand lifted her chin and she flinched. A flick of annoyance whipped across his gaze, but he said, 'I left a message telling you to take it easy, so you did. I won't fire you for it.'

Gillian jerked her chin away. His touch wreaked havoc on the regularity of her heartbeats. 'So what if you do? I'll get myself another job—with a rival antique firm. Then I'll tell them all your secrets.'

'You disloyal little bitch!' He moved nearer, so that she had to tilt her head right back to look at him. He gripped her upper arms. 'I do believe you would.'

She stared him out, but her thoughts were chaotic. Their renewed intimacy had brought her body back to life. Now, to her consternation, it clamoured for more, and yet more, of his love. 'You don't know me very well, do you?' Her voice, annoyingly, had wavered.

He had not seemed to notice. 'But I should have known, shouldn't I? I said once before you don't know the meaning of the word "loyalty". First to me, four years ago, then to Everett's first wife, whom you cheated by producing *his* offspring, even while he was married to her. Again, more recently, when you allowed me to make love to you, even though you're now engaged to the man—who also happens to be the father of your child.'

Wrenching out of his grasp, Gillian stared up at him, hating yet loving him, loving his thick brows and strong facial structure, the squareness of his jaw, even while the fury in his eyes made her coldly afraid. It came to her like a blow in the stomach and she crumpled mentally—she didn't care any more about convention.

It didn't matter that he was an engaged man and she, supposedly, an engaged woman—she wanted to be rocked in those strong arms, to feel her skin against the roughness of his chest, to experience again the manliness of him.

Even as she heard herself cry, 'Why must we quarrel like this? Why must you always be so angry with me?' she knew she should have stayed silent. But the words were out, hanging on the air. Then, to her own surprise, her arms were round his neck, holding on to him. And she was a child, desperate for love, terrified of being left behind for ever.

'Stay with me,' she heard herself crying, and there was a ringing, childlike voice in her ears, 'don't ever go away!'

There was a muttered curse, a brutal hand reaching behind and tearing her arms from him. And she knew what it was like to be Gary.

At the door, he turned, walking slowly back. 'What am I doing—walking away from such an invitation? I must be crazy!' His arms went round her, imprisoning and savage, and she came to her senses in time to stiffen. Randall said, 'Oh no, you don't. You were glad enough for me to take you before, easing your physical needs. Now you'll ease mine.'

This time it was she who was wrenching herself free, even though the pain of the struggle made her wince and gasp for breath. He let her go in the end, facing her with blazing eyes, hands spread on hips, jacket pushed back.

'You callous, vindictive brute!' she accused. 'I *hate* the man you've become. I wish you'd never come back into my life. I'd rather have spent the rest of my days loving the *memory* of you.'

'Too bad for you, my beautiful lover, that I'm still on this earth. You'll just have to get used to the idea, won't you, because even when you're married to Everett Bushell, I'll be around. I'll be around because this is *my* business, your livelihoods are in *my* hands. So you'll dance to *my* tune, both of you, otherwise you'll both be joining the ranks of the unemployed.'

Gillian lifted her head proudly. 'At least,' she asserted, knowing even as she said it that it would not apply to her, 'we'll have Everett's house. We'll have a roof over our heads.'

'Did Everett forget to tell you?' he answered nastily. 'I bought his house along with the company. Which means he's my tenant, too.'

Randall's mood next morning was remote. He worked in the downstairs office, catching up on the paperwork. As lunchtime approached, he called Gillian in and told her that he had more work for her to do for him that afternoon.

Even as he spoke, the telephone rang. Randall listened, nodded and said, 'Right, Isobel, stay home and nurse your headache.'

'I'll be all right tomorrow, Randall,' Gillian heard her say. 'These things usually last only a day with me.'

'Good. See you then.' Randall rang off and swung in the chair to face Gillian. 'Cancel the instructions about working for me. Isobel can't make it to the shop today. I want you down here this afternoon. Understand?'

Gillian nodded, pursing her lips at his tone. Once, she would have hit back verbally. After last night the bitterness between them was so strong in the atmosphere, she could almost taste it.

It was near to closing time when the family entered—mother, father and young son. Their faces seemed vaguely familiar, but in the moment Gillian had before they spoke, she had no time to place them.

They were interested in a large piece of furniture and, probably sensing that Gillian needed assistance, Randall emerged from the office. It was a Welsh dresser in which they were interested. Randall had himself purchased the item in London, having had it transported to the shop by road.

'It's not reproduction, it's a genuine antique,' he told the husband and wife, 'dating from about the late eighteenth century.' Blue and white Willow Pattern plates had been placed on it to enhance its warm, pine colour. It did not take them long to decide to buy it.

It was while the man was writing out the cheque for the required amount that the little boy looked fully at Gillian. The child frowned, as if in the effort of remembering, then he smiled. It was his smile that told Gillian all she had wanted to know about where she had seen the family—and especially the little boy—before.

Her thoughts whisked her back to the view with the railings, the benches for people who wished to rest. His name, he had told her, sitting next to her, was Duncan. His sister's name was Lindy. He had asked her for her name and she had told him.

Gillian's heart began to pound. How much longer would it take the father to produce his bank card, proving his identity? When would the little boy stop staring at her? Could she just slip out, unnoticed, until they had gone? But who could escape those piercing young eyes, belonging to the child who had reminded her so much of her own son?

At last the man had finished. Randall was satisfied and so were the customers—all but the child. The parents moved to the door. 'Come *on*, Duncan,' his father said.

The boy stood stock still. 'You're the lady who sat next to me on that seat. I know your name. It's Gilly.' She remembered she had shortened the name for him.

'Yes, yes,' she said. 'Isn't it strange that you should remember it? 'Bye now, Duncan.'

Duncan stood his ground. 'You've got a little boy,' he asserted. Her breathing was quickening. 'And you're a mummy.' Again she nodded, noting how moist her clenched hands had grown. 'You told me,' Duncan went on relentlessly—would he never stop?—'that his daddy had left him. His daddy had—gone for ever!' His large eyes grew rounder and he ran for comfort to his father's side. '*My* daddy won't leave me.' The words he had spoken before. . . .

'Duncan,' his father reproved, 'whatever's got into you? What are you talking about?'

'I'm so sorry,' the mother apologised. 'He says such funny things sometimes.'

They waved and left, the small boy called Duncan still clinging to his father's hand.

Gillian's face went paper-white. Her mouth felt as parched as if she were lost, without water, in a desert. Swiftly she turned to face the man at her side.

'The child's not yours.' Her voice was high-pitched with fear. 'That little boy Duncan—he was making it up.'

Randall's face was pale, his eyes deadly cold. He walked towards her, each step measured. His hand shot out to grip her wrist and he pulled her with him to the door. He bolted it and turned the 'Open' sign to 'Closed'.

In a swift movement he caught her other hand in his, put them both behind her back, and propelled her forward to the foot of the stairs.

'Walk,' he ordered, and she walked, each step upwards bringing her nearer to the reckoning.

This is the end, Gillian told herself, this is where I must face the inevitable and say my goodbyes to my child, to part of myself. But was it? A flicker of hope burned, turning into a flame. Couldn't she brazen it out, at least until——

They had reached the living-room and Randall swung her round. She tried to free her wrists. 'You're hurting,' she said, summoning defiance.

'So what? You've hurt me like hell—in the past. And if you don't tell me the truth now, I'll put my hands round your lovely neck and—yes, you might well look scared.'

He jerked her against him. His face was so close his breath became her breath, his twisted lips grazed hers. 'Because, my own, I'm growing very, very angry with you. It seems that, three times over, you're a liar. First, the child was Everett's and his ex-wife's. Then the child was Everett's and yours. Now you tell me the child isn't mine. What am I supposed to glean from that statement?'

He lifted her wrists backwards and away from her body, straining her arm muscles until she had to swallow a scream. He went on, 'Everett hasn't "gone for ever", so the boy can't be his and his ex-wife's. Nor, for the same reason, can he be Everett's and yours. Which means there's only one other possibility, since *I'm* the one you assumed, because of that illness I had, to have "gone for ever". So whose child is he?' His face, in his anger, was a contorted, devilish mask. '*Whose child is he?*'

CHAPTER NINE

THE pain in her over-stretched arm muscles blotted out rational response. 'Mine,' she screamed, 'mine! Do you understand? The man—the man who. . . . He was m-married and a—a passing fancy. I've—I've even forgotten his name. After I—I got away from you, I—I missed the——' The what? she thought wildly.

His words, she'd used his words. 'The physical release. It's only natural, isn't it?' She closed her eyes on the face she loved, twisted now with contempt and—yes, she was certain—hatred. She had to insert a smile. After all, she was being brazen, wasn't she? The smile stretched her mouth. It must, she reflected, have looked ghastly. 'A man's not the only one who——' she swallowed convulsively, 'who feels such things.'

Randall let her go and the release from pain hurt as much as the wrenched muscles. Her gasp seemed to please him. 'You corrupt, profligate little bitch!'

Had he really believed her? Had she managed to sidetrack him? And had she protected Gary from Randall's grasp—and from being a pawn in his loveless marriage to June? And if so, at what terrible cost to herself?

She followed up the deception by saying, her eyes reckless, 'Aren't you glad now I ran away from you four years ago? Aren't you profoundly relieved you escaped my clutches?'

A muscle fixed in his jaw. 'You goad me, you little tramp, and you'll discover what it's really like to be used—and abused—by a man. In fact,' he reached out, catching her by the shoulder and jerking her towards him, 'what's wrong with here and now, since you already belong to me. Renewing our—acquaintance the other night has whetted my appetite for more. So——'

From somewhere in the distance came the ringing of the telephone. It jolted them both with its suddenness, its normality. It broke through the tension and the passionate demands with imperious demands of its own. Randall swore, releasing her.

'Don't go away,' he smiled unpleasantly. 'I haven't finished with you yet. There's a piece or two in the jigsaw missing and I won't rest until the picture's complete.' The phone went on ringing.

'Two pieces,' Gillian filled in as Randall moved to the door, 'Everett—for me, and June—for you. Or have you forgotten we've got our own respective partners? The past is gone, and in any case, my past is my own. It's not yours to worry about.' She was calling after him now.

'That's what you think,' he shouted back. 'Just stay there and wait for me. I might be some time. It's a call from New York, otherwise I'd tell them to call back later. Much later!'

As he disappeared, Gillian ran into her bedroom. She grabbed a case, piled into it as many belongings as she could manage and told herself not to panic. Checking in her handbag that she had sufficient money—also that Everett's letter was there, since she could not risk Randall's finding it and discovering that Everett was no longer her future husband—she pulled on a coat.

Without bothering to look in the mirror or even to comb her hair, she crept down the stairs, opened the door to the street and went out, closing it quietly behind her.

As soon as she stepped on the train to London, she knew she was safe. In her apartment she had left no trace of Eve's address, no clue as to the whereabouts of Gary, nothing, in fact, to tell Randall where she might be found.

Except—the train jerked and clattered over points as she remembered—she had informed him herself when he had phoned Eve's house and told her to return to the shop the time she had gone racing to Gary's bedside. No, she decided, sitting back but clutching her bag as though her life depended on it, she had not really told him. Yorkshire, she'd said, a fairly long drive from York itself. . . .

Anxiety began to gnaw again at her mind. Who had given him Eve's number? It must have been Everett. He wasn't there now and, in any case, she had sworn him to secrecy over Eve's address.

Gillian had called Eve from London telling her briefly the reason for her race northwards and the time, roughly, at which she would be arriving. Now, on Eve's doorstep, Gary was welcoming her with open arms and shouts of joy.

'Jimmy'll be home soon,' said Eve, 'and I've made supper for four. He'll be surprised to see you.'

Gillian bent down and hugged her son, putting her cheek against his and holding him as if he were about to be torn from her arms. At last he was content to stay in the living-room while she joined Eve in the kitchen.

'I'm scared, Eve,' Gillian confessed. 'I told Randall a string of—well, lies. I hated doing it but, in the circumstances, that seemed the only way of putting him off the scent. He's ruthless, Eve, and I'm certain that if he so much as guessed the truth about Gary, he'd scent me out and come and take him away.'

'We-ell, I told Jimmy about it—hope you don't mind,' Eve added quickly, and looked relieved as Gillian shook her head, 'and he said if he were Randall he'd want the boy, but—typical man is Jimmy!—he'd want you, too.'

Gillian smiled weakly. 'Nice of him to compliment

me, but——' the fear was in her eyes and Eve seemed to sense that nothing she could say would shift it, 'but Jimmy's not Randall. Don't forget Randall's engaged, and honestly, Eve, I'm not being bitchy, but June's *awful*. Even Everett, when he'd only had to spend a day with her, came back exhausted and saying he didn't know how Randall could even contemplate marrying the woman.'

Eve laughed. 'How's Everett, by the way? I haven't had time to ask——'

'It's over. Everett wrote a long letter—he couldn't stand the tension between Randall and me. He—he said he thought I still loved him, Randall, I mean, and——'

'Do you, Gillian?' Eve was frowning, looking concerned.

Gillian nodded. 'I've never stopped,' she stated dully. 'But what's the use? He's going to marry someone else, quite soon, I think. They've bought a house, ordered the furniture.'

'Gillian,' Eve turned from the sink, 'if Randall's so interested in Gary, surely that's your trump card? You could say, Either you give up your fiancée and marry me, which means that Gary will belong to both of us, or you forfeit Gary for ever?'

Gillian shook her head. 'I'd never blackmail him into marrying me. Also, I'd never use Gary in that way. And—Eve, I want love from a man I marry, love like you've got from Jimmy.'

'Sorry, love,' Eve turned away, 'stupid of me. But I wish I knew of a way to help you. Anyway, you're safe here for the moment, aren't you?'

'Well, Randall doesn't know the address. And he's got to look after the shop, what with Everett still away and Isobel only coming in afternoons.'

Gary came in, shouting, 'Here's Jimmy! His car's outside.' Then he threw himself at his mother and it was the welcome all over again.

Jimmy came in looking surprised. 'Nice to see you, Gillian. How come you're in these parts?'

'Complications,' his wife answered succinctly. 'Tell you later.'

'Ah.' Jimmy looked down at the small boy, who would not let his mother go.

'I hope you don't mind, Jimmy,' Gillian apologised, 'but I had to make a——'

'Quick getaway. Okay, tell me later. Hallo, love.' He seized his wife in a lingering kiss and Gillian turned away, a lump in her throat. In her present unhappy circumstances, to see such affection between husband and wife moved her almost to tears. It was something she had to acknowledge that she would never herself have.

It was a happy meal. Even Gary laughed a lot and cleaned his plate which, Eve said, was unusual. He'd been picking at his food lately. 'Pining, maybe?' she asked.

'You're probably right,' Gillian conceded, 'but I'm here now and not likely to leave him for a long time. I'll find a couple of rooms somewhere, or get a job and rent a flat.'

'Secretarial, aren't you?' Jimmy asked. 'Good at it too, according to Eve. I know someone who needs an efficient secretary——'

The shrill ring of the telephone cut across the conversation. Eve looked at Jimmy, then at Gillian. 'I'll go,' she said.

'Don't look so scared, Gillian,' Jimmy patted her hand across the table. Gary immediately grabbed the patted hand for himself. 'You're safe here.'

Gillian concentrated on Eve's subdued voice in the hall. Then she came in. 'I think it's him,' she whispered. 'I could have told him you're not here, but sorry, love, not even for you could I tell an outright lie.'

Gillian's hand was shaking as she picked up the receiver. Randall must have heard the action followed by her quick, frightened breaths, because he said, 'Gillian?' His voice was sharp, irritated.

She stayed silent, just listening, but he did not repeat her name.

'Mummy,' a small voice piped in the background, 'who is it? Why don't you talk? It—it could be my daddy, Mummy, the one you said——'

Even before Gillian had time to slam down her receiver, she heard the one at the other end clatter into place. Gary was still holding her hand when she returned to the dining-room. 'He heard Gary,' she said, her face white. 'I didn't speak, but,' with a nervous jerk of her head downwards at Gary, 'I didn't need to, did I? If he finds out your address——'

'How will he do that?' Eve queried. 'Have you ever told him my surname? No? Or where I live? Then it's going to be an almighty difficult job tracing you here.'

'It could be done,' Jimmy asserted thoughtfully, 'and if he's as determined as you say, then he'll move mountains to find out.'

'Eve, what can I do?'

It was only when Gary squeaked, 'Mummy, you're hurting!' that Gillian realised how tight her hold was on his hand. She bent down and 'kissed it better' at his request.

'Go somewhere else,' Jimmy suggested. 'Got any friends, relatives, who might take you in?'

Gillian shook her head, then her eyes came to life. 'Martin, my brother—he lives in Darlington, or rather, a town near it. I'll go there. Randall hardly knows him. I haven't seen him for ages, but he'd give us shelter for a while.'

Jimmy was already scanning the train timetable. 'Trains from York, Friday evening. It's not difficult, but you'd have to get a bus or taxi to wherever he lives.'

It took longer than Gillian anticipated getting to her brother's house. He rented the upstairs floor of a two-storeyed house built in a modern development. The place was new to Gillian and the tidiness of the garden and the whole area was so alien to her remembered idea of her brother's character, she wondered at first if she had come to the right place.

It was getting dark and Gary whispered that he was tired. Gillian lifted him and his small arm went round her neck. The suitcase and tote bag rested on the step beside them. The door opened and a tall young man with light brown hair, T-shirt and jeans frowned down at them. The similarity of feature and colouring between the young man and the young woman at whom he looked was unmistakable.

When recognition dawned, the young man's chest expanded and he let out a 'Wow!' which must have been heard, Gillian thought, by the whole neighbourhood. 'If it isn't my big little sister, plus her big little offspring! Well, I'll be—Come in, both of you.'

'Thanks, Martin.' Gillian's voice was thin with fatigue.

They stood on the doormat while Martin carried in the cases. He put them down and crouched to Gary's height. 'Hi, little feller,' he said. 'The last time I saw you was when you were a scrap of a human being. You're a big feller now, my lad, compared with then.'

Gary hid his face in Gillian's coat. Martin straightened. He looked so tall Gillian smiled. 'Last time I saw you,' she remarked, 'you were going through the usual teenage agonies.'

He laughed loudly. 'Got over them long ago. I'm a big boy now.'

'Got a full address book to prove it?' Gillian asked.

'Overflowing. The girls—they come and go. You know how it is.' He gave a big wink at the tiny boy who gazed up at him, apparently unable as yet to work out whether he was friend or foe.

'Oh,' said Gillian. 'Have we come at an awkward

time? I mean, is there a girl in occupation?'

'You're in luck—I'm between girls.' He seized the cases, then dropped them. 'Hey, don't take that literally!'

Gillian laughed and Gary, seeming more secure now, laughed too, without knowing why. Upstairs, Gillian looked round. 'This is an improvement on the last time I saw you. Environs of London, district doubtful, occupying one room in a shared, Victorian house.'

Martin nodded. 'I've moved up the scale a bit. Reasonable job, reasonable money. Enough to keep me in food, clothes, rent—plus anyone who might be passing through.'

She smiled. 'I never thought my little brother's morals would sink to such depths. Girls by the dozen——'

'Hey, you're a good one to talk about morals!' He saw her instant change of expression. 'Sorry about that.' He frowned and looked down at the smiling, trusting little boy who seemed to have taken a liking to him. Crouching down again, he said, 'Hey, Gary, know who I am?' Gary solemnly shook his head. 'I'm your uncle.'

Gary frowned. It was a new word. He tried to say it correctly but failed. Martin taught him in about ten seconds. 'But just call me Martin. Now,' he looked around, 'food.' He looked at Gillian. 'Then what? A bed for the night?'

'The floor would do for me, Martin, plus a sleeping bag. Gary might be better in a bed, but——'

'No trouble. Bed in the bedroom—naturally. Folding bed for the boy next to it. A couch for me in the living-room.'

'That's good of you, Martin. I don't want to put you out. I wouldn't have come, but—well, it's an emergency.'

'It is?' He frowned, started to speak, then changed

his mind. 'I won't ask questions.'

They went into the bedroom. '*Double* bed, Martin?' Gillian pretended to be shocked.

'Goes with the house.' He grinned. 'Comes in useful at times—like now.' Another wink at Gary. 'Most of the stuff's not mine.'

He took them into the kitchen. 'I can open a few tins. What does the little feller like?'

'No food, thanks, Martin. We had a few sandwiches on the train. A glass of milk for Gary would be fine.'

'Ah, milk. Now that I'd have to borrow. The bloke downstairs lives on it, I'll go and buy a bottle off him.' He was gone before Gillian could thank him.

'Come on, darling,' Gillian coaxed Gary. 'Here's Martin's bathroom. I'll get the towel Aunty Eve lent us and your pyjamas.'

As she washed him, deciding he was too tired for a bath, he commented on the smallness of the room compared with Aunty Eve's, the cold towel rail—hers was hot, he said—and the lack of rubber ducks to float in the bath.

Martin appeared, having overheard the last comment. 'If I'd known you were coming, Gary,' he laughed, 'I'd have looked out my old one. I've still got it somewhere.'

'You haven't!' Gillian exclaimed, then received one of her brother's large winks.

It was when Gary was tucked up in bed and Gillian and her brother were drinking coffee that she asked him if they could stay for a week or so. He frowned at the request, and she immediately said,

'If you'd rather we found somewhere else, please say so. Jimmy—Eve's new husband—says his parents would take us for a while. They've got a house in York, and——'

'Stay a week or so, with pleasure,' he answered. 'But I wish you'd tell me what it's all about.'

Gillian was silent for so long, Martin went on, 'This

is where we came in, isn't it? I remember, way back, when you came to stay with me in London. You said you were running away. Are you on the run again?'

'In a way,' Gillian answered at last. 'Yes, yes, I guess I am.' She looked at him over the mug from which she was drinking. 'You were the only one who'd help me. Mum and Dad, when they heard about Gary—well, that was the end of the road for them and me.'

Martin nodded. 'I know they never took to Rand.'

At the sound of Randall's name, shortened, as in the past, Gillian winced, but Martin did not seem to notice. 'They threw him out of the house—with your aid.'

Now it was his turn to wince. 'Sorry about that, but in those days I had to do what I was told. I didn't like it, Gilly.' She warmed even more to him as he used her nickname from the past.

'All the same, I doubt if Randall's forgiven you. He certainly hasn't forgiven me—for running away, I mean.'

Martin looked puzzled. 'You're talking in the present tense. I thought he'd just about come to the end of the road, so to speak? I—er—thought he had no future.'

'I should have told you. Randall was cured. He's completely healthy now. I know because he turned up in our lives again, Everett's and mine.' She explained the whole story, up to that moment. 'I'm scared, Martin, scared that if he ever catches up with me, he'll take Gary away from me. You see, after I'd married Everett—which, as I've told you, I'm now not going to—Everett was intending to adopt Gary.'

Martin was silent, as if trying to work things out. He said at length, 'What made you come here?'

Gillian told him about Randall's phone call to Eve's house, how Gary had talked when she had not, and how Randall probably heard him. 'So I left Eve's place and made for the only person I could think of who'd help me.' She looked at him, putting down her mug. 'I couldn't go to Mum and Dad's, Martin. I've written a few times and had rather stilted answers from Mum——'

'That was because Dad read them.'

Gillian felt herself near to tears. 'Mum could have phoned, even if it was just to say "How are you?"' The tears overflowed and Martin got up, putting an awkward arm across her shoulders. Then he sat down and left her to cry. When she mumbled an apology, he said,

'That's okay. You're tired. You've been through a lot lately.' When her handkerchief was pushed into a pocket, she managed a smile. 'Look, Gilly, take my advice. Go and see them some time. I know in my bones they'd love to see you and the little lad. He's their only grandchild. I can tell you, they'll love him on sight. He's an endearing little chap—I've taken to him myself.'

Gillian smiled at the colour in her brother's cheeks. Then she said, 'Even Dad?'

'Even Dad. The moment that child calls him "Grandpa", he'll melt like ice in a heatwave.'

Later, in bed, listening to her son's regular breathing, Gllian recalled Martin's words. One day, she promised herself, before very long, she would go and see her parents. And even if she did receive a rebuff—although she knew her mother would open her arms—it would still have been worthwhile, if only to have a sight of her parents' faces again.

With a sigh she turned on to her side and slept.

'Mummy, Mummy!' Gary's high-pitched squeal and the leaping weight of his body all over the bed had her coming to startled wakefulness. 'This isn't Aunty Eve's house, so you must get up and get the breakfast.'

Gillian smiled at his very male assumption, assimiilated at an alarmingly young age, that a woman's place was in the kitchen.

'It's Martin's house,' she pulled the pillow over her head to protect her face from his smacking kisses, and felt his young fists pummelling it, 'so *he* must get the breakfast.' Her voice was muffled.

Gary still bounced about the bed, then, when the assault and battering had stopped, she breathed a sigh of relief. 'Is it safe to come out now?' she asked. There was no answer, and she wondered if he was frightened. Children sometimes were, she knew, if they could not see their mother's face. She removed the pillow, said, 'Here I am,' and stopped, her eyes widening in fear, turning to a primitive terror.

She was gazing at a man, tall, hair roughened, shirt open to the waist, dark shadows beneath his piercingly blue eyes. His face was hard, the line of his mouth even harder.

'No,' she whispered, 'no! It can't be you. It's a nightmare——'

'Thanks a lot,' Randall drawled, then his eyes went to the boy who was kneeling, hands piled on his head, staring. 'Hi, Gary.' The hard mouth had softened.

Gary scrambled to sit on the side of the bed. 'You,' he whispered, 'you're my daddy. My daddy!' His voice had risen to a squeak, then it lowered, wavering as he gazed harder, 'Aren't you?'

Randall pulled a photograph from his pocket. The frame, smashed as the glass had been from his hurling it across the room, had gone. 'You took it,' Gillian whispered, 'you took it from beside my bed.'

'That's me,' Gary said. 'So,' his eyes grew bright and wondering as at a new toy, 'you *are* my daddy.'

'Which makes you my son. Right, Gillian?' His back was to her.

'Right, Randall,' she choked, then reached for the wrap at the foot of the bed. Randall turned quickly, taking the wrap from her. 'Randall, let me have it!'

The door was partly open and her voice had risen.

'Sh-sh! Not in front of the children.' Martin was in the doorway, grinning.

Gillian half sat up, which was as far as Randall's weight on the side of the bed would allow. 'Martin, you traitor! You miserable, rotten little——'

'Not so much of the little,' Martin said blandly. 'I'm bigger than you.'

'You let me down!' she shrieked. 'I'll never forgive you for that. I trusted you. I'll never trust you again!'

'Hey, little feller,' Martin ignored his sister's abuse, 'grab your clothes and let's get dressed together. Then we'll wash, in the bathroom that's too small, the towel rail that isn't hot, and there's no rubber ducks to float. Let's leave your mummy and daddy,' his grin widened and his voice dripped syrup as he used the emotive words, 'to kiss each other "hallo".'

Gary, joining in what appeared to him to be the fun, did as his uncle suggested and followed him out. At the door, however, he turned. 'You're my daddy,' he stated, and the statement was unequivocal. He ran off.

'Give me my wrap,' Gillian's hand came out.

'No. How come he's so sure about me?'

Gillian was silent.

Randall twisted sideways on the bed, to face her. 'Tell me or I'll throttle you.' With his fatigue-shadowed eyes, the unshaven shadow around his cheeks and jaw, the dark chest hair, the feel of which she knew so well, he looked capable of doing just that.

She was silent just a moment too long. His hands came at her throat and settled roughly, exquisitely, around it. But instead of pressing, his thumbs started to caress. Swallowing deeply, trying to will her pulsing heart to a slower beat, she answered, 'I thought he'd never see you, as you know, so I showed him a picture of you each time I saw him. It was taken by me one—one day in the park. I think Gary was unsure for a moment just now because you were younger then.'

'And now I'm old, am I? But not too old, as you've discovered, for the things that matter most in life, like making love and loving.'

'I'm glad you agree there's a difference.' If she didn't tear at his hands soon, she would be reaching out for him.

'Ah,' to her relief his hands fell away, leaving the skin of her neck tingling, 'we're back to my darling fiancée, are we?'

Gillian flinched at his description, trying in vain to scent sarcasm. Since it was absent, it surely meant that Randall had developed some kind of affection for June, and that could only mean one thing—that since her own marriage to Everett would not now take place, she had a hard fight on her hands to keep Gary.

Her legs swung from under the bedclothes and Randall looked with interest at the outline of her thighs as the silky material draped over them. Her wrap was back on the bed and this time she flung it round her. Randall's gaze was quizzical as he watched the action. 'You had my child,' he mused. 'No wonder your body had matured beyond belief!'

Hoping to distract him from herself, she asked, 'How did you know where I was? I thought I was safe from you here.'

'It's a long story.' He was plainly not going to enlighten her. 'Why were you running away from me again?'

Her chin lifted defiantly as she threw his own words back. 'It's a long story.' Throwing off the wrap, she began to get dressed, then remembered he was there. 'Would you please go out?'

He wandered across to the window, leaning back against it. 'You're not trying to tell me you're shy? A sleep-around like you?' There was mockery in his eyes. 'First Everett—after all,' the jeer in his voice goaded her, 'Gary is Everett's and yours, isn't he?' His eyebrows rose in mock innocence. 'Or was it yours and an unknown man's, married unfortunately, but willing to oblige, but not, even more unfortunately, eager to acknowledge the progeny he'd fathered?'

'So I invented lovers. But even if I did fabricate—'

'Why not be honest and call them "lies"?' Anger had ousted his tolerant manner. 'Under what name did you register Gary?'

She studied her furry slippers. 'My name—Taylor.'

'Why?'

Gillian met his anger with her own. 'What other name could I use? Since you weren't there to sign the register, nor did you put into writing a statutory declaration that you were Gary's father—either of which, I was told at the time, the law required—he had to be given my own surname.' She played with her slipper with her bare foot. 'I was also told he could eventually be re-registered in the father's name, provided the father subsequently filled in the statutory declaration.'

'Thanks for telling me—now. At the time, I wasn't asked. Nor did I even know. But you know that, don't you? You wanted the whole thing kept secret from me, didn't you? What I'd like to know is why.'

'Mummy, D——' A small, slightly scared face peered round the door and cut the strange word off.

'Gary.' The round, fair-skinned face was lifted to the older face so like his own. 'Come over here.' Randall spoke quietly. Gary obeyed, first glancing at his mother as if for permission. Randall's hands rested gently on his son's shoulders, then he crouched on his haunches. 'Say it, boy. Say that word.' Gary seemed puzzled. Randall prompted him. 'Mummy and——'

'Daddy!' Gary delivered the word as if it were a newly-mined diamond. A small, shy hand stretched out to touch Randall's cheeks, his nose, his mouth.

'Yes, I'm here, lad, all of me. Are you glad?'

There was a moment's hesitation, then two arms wrapped around Randall's neck and clung as if he would never let him go. Gillian turned her head away, hiding the tears which had welled. The wheel has turned full circle, she thought, father and son united. At that moment Gary had, without knowing it, taken one enormous step away from her.

'Hey, you lot, sorry to break up the family circle, but breakfast's ready.'

'But I'm not.' Gillian's voice was muffled by her handkerchief.

'Okay, I'll keep yours hot. Come on, apple of your father's eye—not to mention your mother's.'

'I'm not an apple,' Gary protested, going out with Martin. 'I'm a boy, a big boy. . . .' His voice faded as the living-room door closed.

'Gillian?' Randall stood in front of her. 'Look at me.' She shook her head. His hands fitted under her arms and lifted her to stand against him. Through the thinness of her nightgown the touch of him was electric. His finger lifted her chin. His lips settled momentarily on each of her damp eyes, then moved to her lips.

In seconds she was in his arms, melting into him. He slipped the nightgown from her shoulders, lowered his head and kissed her breasts. At her gasp of delight his embrace grew harder, rougher, and she felt his desire increase with hers.

'You belong to me, do you hear? No matter how many times you run from me, I'll find you. You bore my child, my son. That makes you mine—mine!' He shook her compliant body as if to help her grasp the fact.

'There's June,' she whispered. 'There's—there's Everett. We can never belong.'

'Rand!' Martin was shouting from the kitchen. 'Break it up. Your food's getting cold. Tell your woman hers is keeping hot.'

Randall let her go. 'I'm completing that form of declaration stating I'm Gary's father. He'll be re-registered in my name.'

'Gary's mine, Rand,' she held desperately to his arm. 'That's like taking him away.' He shook himself free, his mood having undergone a frightening change.

'I'm just your woman,' she persevered. 'You heard what Martin called me, and it's true. I'll never be your wife—you as good as told me. You were cured of me, you said—just as I was cured of you.'

He gave her a searing look and left her.

CHAPTER TEN

THERE was one place unused at the table in the corner of the living-room. 'Breakfast's in the kitchen,' Martin shouted from the bathroom. 'Hope it's still hot.'

As Gillian collected it, holding it with an oven glove, she called, 'Where are Gary and Rand?'

'Gone to the shops.' Martin emerged looking damp and clean. 'Rand said something about buying Gary a toy.'

Gillian frowned. 'That's like trying to buy Gary's love. He must know by now he's already got it.'

'For Pete's sake, let him play father while he's here. He's waited long enough, hasn't he?'

'Whose side, Martin?' Gillian enquired over-sweetly. 'Mine or his?'

'Neutral. Look, you loved the man once. You must have, to do what you did, living with him when you knew there was no hope. Or so it seemed. A girl has to be very, very serious about a man when she does that.'

The bacon looked hard, the egg likewise, but she couldn't blame Martin. Anyway, her taste seemed to have deserted her. 'How long is he here for, Martin?' she asked.

Martin shrugged. 'Today, tomorrow—haven't asked.' He returned to the bathroom and came back buttoning his shirt. 'I said we'd join them at the shopping centre.'

Gillian nodded and continued eating. 'Any coffee?'

Martin indicated the pot. 'I made fresh for you.' Gillian thanked him absentmindedly.

A plan was forming in her slightly fevered mind. There was one last chance to get Gary away from Randall. It might work, provided she could manage to act naturally, and provided also that she could tear

Gary away from his new-found father.

Finishing her breakfast, she returned her empty dishes to the kitchen. Martin was washing everyone else's and she promised to help him as soon as she could. He called out, 'No need.' All the same, she hurried back into his bedroom, pushing the door closed.

As quietly as she could, she opened drawers one after the other, but Martin's spare set of car keys were nowhere to be seen. There was one last chance. Feeling like a criminal, Gillian opened the door of his clothes cupboard, holding her breath as the hinge creaked. Slipping her hand in and out of his zipped-jacket pockets, she found them at last.

With a pounding heart she hid the keys in her handbag, closed the cupboard door and, taking a breath, joined her brother in the kitchen. 'Tell me something, Martin,' she said, drying while he washed the breakfast dishes, 'how did Randall know where to find me?'

Martin reddened slightly. 'Guilty, ma'am,' he muttered. 'But it didn't start here.'

Gillian lifted a saucepan. 'Explain yourself, little brother, or I'll hit you so hard you'll——'

'I'll confess.' He dried his hands and slipped them into his jeans pockets. 'Some while ago, I had a phone call. At first I didn't recognise the caller's voice. When he told me his name——'

'Randall West?'

'Rand himself, still alive and very much kicking. He'd seen an advertisement in an antiques magazine about a shop called Bushell's Antiques in Dorset. He wanted a shop where he could invest some of his hard-earned money, collected while he'd been working abroad.'

'Why didn't he tell me all this?' Gillian commented.

'He had his reasons, obviously. Well, then he said he'd heard that my sister Gillian was somewhere in Dorset, too. Did I know where he could find you? I said, well, I didn't know your point of view about him, and he said that didn't matter. He wanted to find you. I told him——' Martin took up a position across the room and grinned at his sister from there—'that it just so happened you were engaged to Everett Bushell who, I understood, owned an antique shop. That was all he wanted to know, I hardly heard his thanks when he'd rammed the phone down. The rest you know.'

'No, I don't. What about him coming here?'

'Er——' Martin pretended to loosen his open collar, 'I was hoping you wouldn't ask. He rang me recently saying his sixth sense told him you were about to make a run for it. He didn't know your son's foster-mother's address, only her phone number.'

'Which he rang. And, as I told you, although I didn't talk, Gary did.'

Martin nodded. 'He heard Gary, knew you'd try to do a disappearing act yet again, and rang me. If by any chance you turned up here, would I give him a ring? We arranged a signal, in case I had no chance to talk. Three rings on the phone, then cut off.'

'So,' she advanced on him, 'when you went downstairs for the milk——'

He was nodding like a small boy, like Gary when he had done something wrong. 'I rang. Sorry, Gilly,' he fended off the hand that threatened his head, 'but personally, I think the whole thing's——'

'Stupid. Think what you like, Martin, but one thing I can tell you. Rand's not taking Gary away from me.'

Martin shrugged and said, 'Let's go.'

As they drove to the shopping centre, Gillian watched Martin's hands manoeuvring the controls. The car was small and easier to manage, she guessed, than Everett's larger model.

A joyful Gary greeted them as they met outside the mock Tudor café in the high street. He carried, as if it were a babe-in-arms, a large box, allowing no one else to take it. 'A garage,' he announced, 'with cars and lorries and shops.'

'Cost a fortune, I bet,' muttered Martin, but Randall, whose face was more animated than Gillian had seen it since the old days, said,

'My son deserves only the best.' His narrowed gaze fell on Gillian.

Was he, she wondered, goading her to declare, 'He's *our* son, not just yours'? If so, she wouldn't give him the satisfaction of responding to his bait. They had coffee and scones and butter and cakes. They occupied a table for four. Randall sat opposite her, with Gary beside him. Martin was next to her, facing Gary.

As she stirred her coffee she watched, through her lashes, her son and his father. It looks just as if Randall's taken possession of Gary already, she thought, fear making her hand shake as she lifted the cup to her mouth. Drinking, she saw over the cup's rim Randall's observant eyes on her. Did he miss nothing? He smiled, but she would not smile back.

Randall's eyes went to Martin. What message was passing between them now? As she remembered Martin's spare car keys, in an act of reassurance, Gillian's foot felt for her handbag, which she had placed between her chair and the table leg. Her foot knocked against another leg, a human one, which followed her own back to its place.

The scrape of his leg against hers brought a pink glow to her cheeks. It was, she told herself severely, the heat of anger, not pleasure. Gary, his mind on his newly-acquired treasure, was absorbed as he drew fresh orange juice into his mouth through a straw. Now and then he took a bite of cake, and Gillian was glad, thinking of the long journey ahead.

As they emerged from the café, she said, 'I'd like to do some shopping. You know,' she smiled at her brother, 'food and things.'

'Food? I've got plenty of that.'

'Oh, but——' she thought of the sandwiches she

must buy, the bottles of lemonade, chocolate to keep them going on the way, 'I must—I must contribute to the meals. Here—here's a supermarket. Come on, Gary. We won't be long,' she threw over her shoulder.

To her dismay, both Randall and Martin followed. 'I'll have to do my share towards the food, too,' Randall told Martin, who shrugged, then nodded.

With great regret, Gillian hurried past all the items she had wanted to buy, carrying the empty wire basket through a checkout at the other end of the store. She coaxed Gary through the rear exit. Outside, she looked left, then right, remembering at last where Martin's car was parked.

Gary was still clutching his parcel, but when Gillian tried to grasp his hand, he protested. She took his parcel from him, against more protests, and pulled him across the busy road, ignoring the blaring horns of angry drivers.

Since Martin's car was yellow in colour, it was easy to find. With shaking hands she unlocked it and put the parcel on the rear seat. Gary scrambled in after it, refusing to be parted from his precious acquisition. The car started at the third attempt, and she reversed out of the parking space. A few moments later she was on her way.

Gillian decided not to take the direct route to Eve's house—not that she was well acquainted with routes of any kind in this area. She had found a map in the door pocket of Martin's car.

Trying to regain her composure after the fears and uncertainties involved in her rush to escape, she considered that the journey south was reasonably straightforward. This was why, after some deliberation, during which Gary tore at the adhesive tape around his parcel, she made the decision to take a more indirect route.

That way, she calculated, even if Randall followed,

it would put him quite off the scent. In any case, he did not even know where Eve lived. When she considered that the villages she was passing through were out of the way enough for her to find somewhere to eat, Gillian pulled the car off the road and led Gary across the quiet village street to a small restaurant.

To her relief, he ate well, relishing the ice cream that followed, but all the time he was worrying to get back to his new toy. After buying packets of food and biscuits and a bottle of lemonade, she filled the tank at the local filling station. It would, she thought, take her a good many miles.

Driving on, she followed the signposts, wishing there were more. The sun had disappeared behind a cloud which was rolling up, taking with it the only means she had of knowing in precisely which direction she was driving. The roads rarely ran straight, the bends were numerous and signs of habitation grew increasingly less the farther she drove.

The moors had opened out long ago, stretching on all sides into the far distance. Gary was showing signs of becoming fretful.

'Where are we going,' he kept asking, 'back to Daddy? To see Martin again?'

'To Aunty Eve's, darling,' she told him, and was taken by surprise when he wailed that he wanted to go back to his daddy.

The rain began as she pulled to the side and found the chocolate she had bought. It kept Gary quiet for a while, then he said he wanted a drink. There was another stop for that. Gillian had given up consulting the map. The signposts and the road numbers did not seem to line up. It was as the rain clouds glowered over the fells, bringing a threat of early nightfall, that she had to admit to herself that she was lost, hopelessly and frighteningly lost.

There were sheep, of course, everywhere she looked. An occasional car sped past. In the distance, at the end of impossibly winding roads, white-painted farmhouses stood. In the mist that was gathering they were, she had to acknowledge, much too far away to ask a weary little boy to walk. She herself had grown tired, too. The tension and driving fear that had kept her going was taking its toll now, and she wanted to do nothing but park the car and sleep.

Seeing a flat area off the road a short distance ahead, she pulled in and bumped to a stop. The silence was so deep, Gary listened and said, 'What's that?'

'Nothing, just nothing,' Gillian answered—and that, she thought, was just about it. Nothingness, for mile upon mile, daunting in its beauty, even under the grey skies of approaching night. Rousing herself, she brought out the food bag again, producing the biscuits and the lemonade. There were also two bags of crisps, one for each.

When all the food had gone and the bag was put away, she searched without much hope in the rear of Martin's car for a rug or old blanket. All she found was an ancient sweater. Joining Gary in the back, she said, 'This is Martin's. It's old, but it's wool and it'll keep you warm.'

'Is it far to Aunty Eve's now, Mummy?' Gary asked in a small, plaintive voice.

'I hope not, darling,' was the only answer she could give him, as she stroked the fine, fair hair. She shivered as the cold air invaded the car, despite the closed windows. Having tried the heating and discovered it was not working, she knew that spending the night in such an unfriendly environment, without adequate covering, was taking a great risk.

Her head rested on Gary's and his breathing became regular with sleep. As long as Gary's warm and safe. . . . It was her last thought before she, too, drifted into a troubled, chilling unconsciousness.

Voices woke her and she recognised them at once.

'What time is it?' That was Randall. 'Two o'clock,' Martin answered.

'Gary, Gary,' she whispered urgently, shaking him awake, 'come on, out of the car.' She had the door open away from the voices, lifting Gary out. He was dazed with sleep, even more than she was. 'Run,' she whispered, 'run as fast as you can!'

The moors were soft beneath their racing footsteps and Gary did his best, but it was only his mother's hand that stopped him from tripping and falling. Her own legs would not obey her and she despaired as the thump of running feet from behind seemed to be gaining on them.

Two strong hands clamped on to her shoulders, forcing her to a stop. Two other hands swung Gary's small, tired body to be held close and told, 'It's okay, little feller, it's your Uncle Martin. We're going home, boy, home—to my home. Your garage? It's there in my car, lad.'

Gillian was struggling with the two arms which were by now wrapped tightly around her. She heard Martin say, 'She found my spare set of keys. I'll take my car, you put her in yours. I'll get the little one to bed. It's a good thing we came this way. That sixth sense of yours must be working overtime! See you, Rand—some time. I wish you luck, mate. Sooner you bring my sister to heel than me!'

By the time there was the sound of a car revving, Gillian found her hands were locked together behind her. The man who had imprisoned her was behind her, too.

'If you think,' she got out, gritting her teeth and glad that her hour or two of rest had renewed her energy, 'you're going to find it easy to get the better of me then you'd better think again!'

Using her locked hands, he spun her round as easily as if she were a spinning top. He did not release her hands.

'Bully!' Her eyes burned up at him in the faint glow from the car headlamps. 'You're a brute, you're a sadist——'

'And you're the most stupid little fool I've ever come across. You've tried this quick getaway trick once too often, Gillian. This is the last time.'

'Of course it is,' her voice was, to her annoyance, thickening with tears, 'you've won, haven't you? You've got Gary. When we get back, I'll find him gone, spirited away by my ever-loving brother, hidden in some place where I can't find him. Martin's on your side—he told me. He's been the link man in all this, hasn't he?'

Her hands were free now and she didn't know what to do with them.

'He's against me, just like all my family's been against me!'

'You're babbling rubbish, Gillian.' His hands settled on her arms but she tore away.

'No, I'm not. You weren't there. I carried your baby—alone. I had your baby, in a hospital, alone. No one to visit, no proud father bringing flowers like all the other mothers. All I had was my baby.'

'Our baby.'

'*My* baby!' Her voice rang out over the moors. She willed her body not to shake with cold. 'My parents disowned me, my brother wasn't allowed near me. He was under age at the time, you see. I was a year and a half over it, so *I* was big enough, in my parents' eyes, to take the full force of the consequences of my terrible action—loving a man enough to have his child.'

Randall started pulling her towards him, but she resisted.

'Yes,' her voice turned nasty, 'I loved you then. Unbelievable, isn't it?'

'Have you ever thought,' his hands found his pockets and he spoke quietly, 'what you deprived me of? You ran away—you're good at that, aren't you?—

telling me nothing, giving me no reason for disappearing from my life. I hunted high and low for you. I even lowered myself to contact your parents, knowing I'd get a dusty answer—as I did. They slammed the phone down on me.'

The silence, as he paused, was a thick blanket around them, loud with its emptiness, bearing no message of hope, but the clouds had cleared.

'I sat for days, trying to work out why, why. . . . I came up with the only answer I could think of—someone had scared you about catching what I had. You didn't like to tell me, so you upped and ran. You hid yourself so well it was as if you'd gone to another planet. So I started to hate you. It ate into me so much that I turned on other women. Yes, I had other women, but by God, I was hard on them!'

His breathing was deep and loud. There was no other sound.

'I imagined all the time, you see, that it was you I had there in bed with me. I was giving you hell. Yet I still couldn't exorcise you.'

'So you've had your revenge, Randall. You made life hell for me. All the time—after you'd come back into my life—I was afraid. Afraid you'd take away the only thing I had left of you, the child I love to distraction. And now you've succeeded.' She turned away, unable to speak because of the unshed tears.

The darkness she faced gave her back no answer. Now and then a sheep bleated. That might be me, she thought, crying for my little one that's been taken away.

'When I'd had the baby,' she went on, 'I had no place to live. I went to a hostel where they took me in with Gary. I scanned the papers and found a couple—not young—who were advertising for help in the home. I wrote quickly, saying I'd got a baby and did they mind? I said I was young and strong and would do anything.'

Randall did not speak. It seemed as if he had even stopped breathing.

'They took me in, that wonderful old couple. They loved Gary as their own great-grandchild—yes, they were that old. They didn't mind him crying in the night. They even got up to soothe him. I'll never meet people like them ever again.'

She turned, but could only see his still outline. 'It wasn't a palace they lived in. It was a little cottage, two hundred years old. But I kept it spotless for them, cooked for them, washed their clothes, dug their garden. I was so glad to have a decent roof over my and Gary's head.'

When his arms came round her at last, she couldn't hold back the tears any longer. He held her gently while she sobbed, then, when she was still, removed his own jacket and put it round her, holding her to him again.

'What happened after that?' he asked quietly.

'The inevitable. The wife first, then, as if he couldn't live without her, the husband. I cried for a week.' There was a long silence. 'I had to get out—relatives wanted the cottage. Then I thought of Eve, an old school friend. We'd kept in touch. She'd lost her husband in a car accident, then lost the baby she was carrying. That's how she came to foster Gary for me, while I went south for work.'

'Is that how you met Everett?'

She nodded. 'I'm sorry for—for what I did, Rand. I'm sorry for depriving you of the pleasure of the sight of your son growing from babyhood to childhood. His first steps, first words. I kept showing him your picture right from the start. You see,' her forehead pressed against his chest, 'I thought you—you—I'd never see you again. If only I'd known you were getting better before I——'

'If only I'd told you. But you see,' he lifted her face and the faint glow from the lamps illuminated her pale features, 'I wanted it to be a surprise.'

'Oh, Randall, I'm so tired, so tired.' He lifted her and carried her to the car, putting her in the back seat and joining her there. His arms went round her and they lay back together, her head on his chest, the hardness of it a pleasure, exhausted though she was. 'I didn't tell you about the baby because I thought you'd be angry. And—and I thought that, by the time he was born, you wouldn't be—around to enjoy him, anyway. So I did the only thing I knew, on the spur of the moment. I ran.'

He seemed to be smiling. 'You're an expert at that, my darling.'

'Now—now there's June, your fiancée. When you apply for custody—you can, you know—your case for keeping Gary will be better than mine. You see, you'll have a wife by then. But I won't have a husband.'

Randall stirred beneath her.

'You're engaged.'

'Not now. Everett wrote to me, said he thought I still loved you——' She checked herself. Would he ask questions? It seemed not.

'I contacted Everett in New York,' he said. 'I had to know the position between you. He told me then that the engagement was off. You might be interested to know, my own, that he told me something else. While you were slaving away working for me, Isobel was spending those evenings with him. He came to like her so much, he's already proposed to her—by telephone across the Atlantic—and she's accepted.'

'Isobel and Everett? Yes, they should go well together. They're both good people. I'm glad.'

'Do you still love him?' Randall's voice had grown distant.

'I never did. Fond of him, but how could I love him, when I loved you? There, now you have it. When—when you marry June,' she strained to see his face but failed, 'if—if you want me as your mistress, darling, I'll—I'll come to you.'

He pulled her fiercely into his arms. 'What the hell kind of man do you think I am? You've just handed out an insult to me so bad that if a guy had said it, I'd have hit him to the other side of the universe.'

'Rand,' she pleaded, 'explain what you mean. Why was that an insult? When a woman loves a man, even if he doesn't love her back——'

'It's your turn to explain yourself, woman. Why the hell did I take a chance on being discovered, and phone your parents when I returned from working overseas?'

'You did? But surely you didn't ask for me?'

'For Martin. I said I was an old friend and didn't have his address. They gave it to me. I contacted Martin, hoping he'd know where you were.'

'He did, but only because we'd kept in touch with the occasional letter.'

'It was enough. I'd seen this advertisement. Something drew me to it. I wanted to know more.'

'Martin told me the rest. Why did you buy Everett's business, Rand? To get your revenge on me? You told me often enough.'

'Revenge? Any more insults?' Randall felt inside his jacket pocket which she still wore, and produced a piece of paper. 'A marriage licence which I bought in Dorset before I left on Thursday. On Monday we return to Dorset. On Tuesday we'll be married.'

'But you haven't even asked me!'

'I'm not asking, I'm making you my wife legally. *De facto*, you've been that for more than four years. Do I make myself clear?'

'No.'

He ignored the statement. 'Today, or was it yesterday, with Gary beside me, I bought two rings. One for you to wear now—two diamonds set in platinum. Give me your hand.' He removed Everett's ring and pocketed it. Then he pushed his own ring into place.

It fitted perfectly. 'The other one is for our wedding day, a plain gold band.'

'I still don't understand,' Gillian told him plaintively. 'There's June.'

'After six months of being engaged to June, I wouldn't marry her if she were gift-wrapped in gold.'

'You mean you continued the engagement just to hurt me and for no other reason? I should be very angry with you, Mr West.' Her words merged into each other with tiredness, plus a mounting happiness.

'Not nearly as angry as I was with you. You and Everett—safe, solid,' his tone was sneering, 'promising you security, whereas I, by contrast, was unreliable, irresponsible——'

'I never said that!'

'Maybe not, but you implied it.'

'Anyway,' she tried deflecting his thoughts, 'you would never have gone through with a marriage to June, I'm sure you wouldn't.'

He put her beneath him and bent over her menacingly. 'What makes you so sure, my own?' The question held a threat.

'Well,' she wriggled under him, but he stilled her with his own weight, 'after what Everett said about her.'

'He told me. Poor Everett! I should never have wished her on him that day.'

'Rand,' she ran her fingers round his roughening cheeks, 'will you furnish your house with antiques after all?'

'Our house. And, my love, the choice will be yours.' He looked through the car windows. 'The clouds have gone. There's a moon and stars out there. But I'm damned if I'm going to make love to you on the rain-soaked moors.'

'Once, Rand, it was the only bed we had. The hard earth, the trees as a covering.... Don't you remember?' she implored. 'The moon, the starlit sky?

Just like it used to be. Or have you forgotten?'

'Forgotten I have not,' he answered forcefully. 'I reminded you of it soon after we met again.'

Gillian nodded vigorously. 'You were like a stranger, Rand.' She put her lips to his chest, inhaling the male aroma of his skin. 'But not now, not any more. I belong to you again just as surely as I did in those days.' She strained to look at the sky, the moon-washed moors. 'It's beautiful out there, darling.'

'My own, are you *asking* me to take you out there?'

'I'm not saying "no",' she answered, smiling, 'and I'm not saying "yes".'

'Right. That's answer enough.' He reached for a rug which was on the floor of the car, opened the door and threw out the rug. He lifted her into his arms and, spreading the rug with his foot, placed her on it, lying beside her. With slow, deliberate movements, he unfastened the buttons of her blouse. She shivered, and it was not entirely caused by the chill air. With shy yet daring fingers she opened his shirt.

He tugged her round on to her side to face him. 'I want to tell you here and now,' he said, 'that I've never once stopped loving you.'

'Nor I you, Rand,' she whispered. She was so close to him the pressure of his chest hurt her breasts, but she did not care.

'No matter how much I cursed and told myself I hated you for running away from me,' he went on, 'that love persisted. Night and day you haunted me. In every woman I looked at, I saw your face. I thought I saw you in crowds—even in foreign countries where my reason told me you could never be.'

'When I ran away, Rand, it was because I'd just discovered that there would be a baby. I thought you were too ill to be burdened with the responsibility. It wouldn't have been fair, I thought. I longed to tell you, but *my* reason told me not to.'

He rubbed his cheek against her hair, then his lips

found her throat. She was beginning to come alive in his arms, arching against him, wanting the strength of him lifting her to the heights they used to share together.

'If only I could explain just what you did to me,' he said huskily. 'Every night I'd reach out to find you, but there was just an empty space in my bed in that lonely room. I needed you, wanted you in my arms. Like now. I wanted you—like I want you now.'

With growing urgency his hands tugged her blouse free and his lips found secret places, teasing her breasts into a yielding fullness. Her body was alight with desire, her love for him all the deeper because she had borne his child.

Their legs entwined and she became aware of the desire that was filling him. She delighted in the familiar touch of his body on hers, loving the feel of his skin against her skimming palms.

Just before their love became complete, he murmured, 'My lover, my only love, soon to be my wife, I warn you—never run away from me again. If you ever did, no matter where you might go, nor how far away, I'd come after you as I did tonight. I'd capture you and make you mine until you cried out for mercy.'

'Now I know you love me back, I'll never run from you,' she promised. 'Darling,' she whispered, 'do you remember how it was before—you and me against the world, against fate itself. We came through, Rand, we came through.'

He lifted his head and gazed at her face, radiant in the moonlight. Then his mouth came down, taking hers with rough, total possession.

Harlequin Plus

A WORD ABOUT THE AUTHOR

Born in London and raised in North Essex, a county in eastern England, Lilian Peake grew to love the countryside, going for long rambling walks and filling a journal with all she observed. She became secretary to a local mystery writer, then embarked upon a journalism career.

From fashion writer with a London magazine, she moved on to a position as advice columnist with yet another magazine, both of which jobs, she feels, contributed to a greater understanding of people.

Until almost the moment she started writing her first novel, Lilian believed that she could not do it. "Then I read a book that challenged me," she said. "I remember thinking, *I could write like that!* So I did."

Today, Lilian Peake is the wife of a college principal. Her interests vary, but reading and listening to music top the list. "And as I do the housework," she admits, "I think about my characters and my plots."